"Romily," James said, "look at me!"

Slowly Romily did so, to find his blue eyes smiling down at her. "I think you're involved with me whether you like it or not," he said. "And something tells me you like it—just a little."

The way they were standing, with their bodies so close together, there could be little doubt of that, and the realization made Romily smile, too. But then the smile faded, and she again lowered her head.

"Romily! I don't want you ever to turn away from me again." James paused, then asked gently, "Who was he? What did he do to you?"

"Why do you want to know?"

"So that I can understand. So that I can help you to forget. To heal the wounds."

But for Romily that was going too far. She wasn't ready to drop her defenses. Especially with her sister-in-law's warnings about James clearly in her mind.

SALLY WENTWORTH began her publishing career at a Fleet Street newspaper in London, where she thrived in the hectic atmosphere. After her marriage, she and her husband moved to rural Hertfordshire, where Sally had been raised. Although she worked for the publisher of a group of magazines, the day soon came when her own writing claimed her energy and time. Her romance novels are often set in fascinating foreign locales.

Books by Sally Wentworth

Don't miss any of our special offers. Write to us at the following address for information on our newest releases.

Harlequin Reader Service
901 Fuhrmann Blvd., P.O. Box 1397, Buffalo, NY 14240
Canadian address: P.O. Box 603,
Fort Erie, Ont. L2A 5X3

SALLY WENTWORTH

tiger in his lair

Harlequin Books

TORONTO • NEW YORK • LONDON
AMSTERDAM • PARIS • SYDNEY • HAMBURG
STOCKHOLM • ATHENS • TOKYO • MILAN

Harlequin Presents first edition July 1987
ISBN 0-373-10997-0

Original hardcover edition published in 1986
by Mills & Boon Limited

CHAPTER ONE

SO this was Abbot's Craig. Romily pulled the car into the side of the road and sat back in her seat, wondering for the hundredth time whether she'd done the right thing in coming here. But London had been intolerable and this offer of a job had come along at just the right moment. Or so it had seemed at the time. Then, Romily had felt so heartbroken and bitter that all she'd wanted to do was to get as far away as possible from her job and the people she knew; she hadn't given a thought to Abbot's Craig's remoteness in the Scottish Highlands. But if it was being turned into a hotel then presumably some people must come to the area.

From here, high up on the hill road, she could look down on to its pseudo-Gothic gabled roofs and turrets, on mellow brick walls and latticed windows set into stone mullions. It looked imposing enough, built at the height of the Gothic revival by a rich Victorian as a hunting-lodge, but now too costly for an ordinary family to maintain even as their main home, which was why Romily's brother and sister-in-law, Gerald and Carol Bennion, had decided to turn the place into a hotel after Carol had inherited it from her father at the end of last year. And they had asked Romily to take over the kitchens.

It was a job she was quite capable of doing; she had no qualms about that. She had all the qualifications and experience it needed, and it would, in fact, be a step down after her last job, but

it was only after she had committed herself that
Romily began to wonder if it was a very wise move.
She sighed, feeling fed up and not looking forward
to the future at all, but then the weak March sun
came reluctantly from behind a bank of cloud and
shone on to the house, turning the windows into a
thousand sparkling diamonds. The thick fir trees
surrounding the house lost their sombre hues, and
she glimpsed the blue waters of a lake down below
in the valley. Her heart lifted a little. Maybe it
wouldn't be so bad after all. The scenery, at any
rate, was on a grand scale. Lifting her eyes to look
further up the steep, craggy hillside, thick with fir
trees, Romily glimpsed another building about a
mile further on. This, too, looked to have high,
turreted walls, but these appeared to be the
battlements of a real castle from what she could see
of it among the trees.

The sun went in again, making the landscape
bleak and inhospitable, Romily shivered and
started the car, looking forward to a hot drink and a
soak in a bath after the long drive from London. A
little further on she came to a side turning to the left,
marked by a board with 'Abbot's Craig Hotel'
painted in rough letters on it. Presumably Gerald
hadn't got round to erecting a proper sign yet.
Which made Romily wonder just how near he was
to being ready to open on the date he'd given her.

When she drove down the road and reached the
house her misgivings deepened. There were piles of
builders' materials and tools in the courtyard, even
a bath standing rather forlornly waiting to be
installed. The front door stood wide open and from
inside there came the sound of hammering and an
electric drill. Well, at least something was going on.

Getting out of the car, Romily stretched her cramped legs as she looked round the garden in the fading light. It looked neglected and overgrown, but the basics were there: a good layout and plenty of shrubs to give colour, but the nicest thing about it was the view down the steep hillside to the lake and the rugged peaks on the other side.

'Thought I heard a car. Hallo, Romily. How are you?'

Romily turned at the sound of her brother's voice. It was the first time she'd seen him in over two years and he seemed to have changed, got older. Not that she knew him very well. He was her elder by fifteen years and was actually only her half-brother. They had the same father but different mothers, and hadn't been brought up together. The last time she'd seen him had been at their father's funeral when Gerald had flown back from the Middle East where he'd been working, but when Carol's father left her Abbot's Craig they had decided to return to Scotland.

'Hallo, Gerald. I'm fine, thanks.'

He didn't kiss her or anything, they weren't that close, and Romily was glad of it; right now she didn't want a close relationship with anybody, even a brother.

'I'll take your cases in.'

She unlocked the back of the car and Gerald lifted out her two large cases. 'Is this all?' he asked in some surprise.

'Yes, that's it. Just two cases.'

He looked at her for a moment, then carried them through the wide doorway into the hall, which again was cluttered with ladders and tins of paint.

'How's it going?' she asked doubtfully.

'Oh, coming along, you know.' But he didn't sound at all optimistic. 'Come and say hallo to Carol.'

Leaving her cases at the bottom of the stairs, Gerald led her through a swing door into what must have been the servants' quarters of the house and along a corridor to the huge kitchen. Her sister-in-law was standing at a small electric cooker, trying to prepare a meal in a room strewn with pieces of new equipment that hadn't yet been installed: two large freezers, a commercial cooker, a dishwasher and lots of cartons and crates that hadn't yet been unpacked.

'Romily! Am I glad to see you.' There was a note of genuine relief in Carol's voice and she had no reserves about greeting her with a kiss, but Romily knew that with Carol it didn't mean anything, she greeted everyone she knew like that. 'As you can see, we're in a state of chaos,' she said with a laugh and a wave of her hand round the room. 'We're depending on you to set it all to rights for us. Did you have a good journey? I expect you're hungry. Dinner won't be long. Would you like a sherry first? Find her one, will you, Gerald?'

Romily had opened her mouth to answer the first question, then shut it again as Carol had gone on without a break. It had been such a long time that she had forgotten that this was Carol's normal mode of conversation.

'How are the boys?' she asked, as soon as she could get a word in.

'Oh, they're fine. It's lovely to be near them again, although unfortunately they won't be coming for Easter because they've arranged to go skiing with their school.'

'That's a shame.' There was surprise in Romily's voice; because Gerald had worked abroad, his two sons had been sent to boarding-school in England and she had thought that the family would have taken every opportunity to be together now that they were back in Britain. As the boys' aunt she had conscientiously visited them at school every term and reported back to their parents, but she felt no closer to the boys than she did to Gerald and Carol. They had always accepted her politely enough and quite enjoyed showing off their young and pretty aunt to their friends, but that was as far as it went. Only once or twice with the younger boy, Simon, had Romily ever felt the slightest emotional bond. On one occasion when she'd visited them he had clung to her hand when she was about to leave, and once he'd written her a letter and put 'With love from Simon' and a big 'X' on the bottom. But that was at the beginning, when he'd first been sent to school at the age of five, and he had soon stopped writing at all.

The three of them ate dinner at a small table pushed against a wall in the kitchen, which was about the only available space. The food was all right, but Carol was no cook and didn't pretend to be. Most of her life, here before she was married and out in the Middle East, she had had servants to do the cooking and everything else for her. Presumably she expected to run the hotel on the same lines as she had organised her servants, but if she didn't intend to do any work herself . . . Romily pulled herself up short. She mustn't prejudge. Maybe both Carol and Gerald were willing to work hard to make the hotel a success.

'You said you wanted to open in time for Easter,'

she reminded them. 'Do you think you'll be ready by then?'

'We'll have to be,' Gerald said rather grimly. 'I admit things haven't gone quite as well as we'd planned. Late deliveries and running into snags with the bathroom conversions, that kind of thing, but we must have at least four rooms ready by Easter because I've taken bookings for them.'

Romily looked from one to the other of them, saw the frown and tiredness around Gerald's eyes and heard the note of strain in Carol's overbright chatter. Things obviously weren't going well for them and it was beginning to show. She smiled encouragingly. 'Well, now that I'm here you'll have an extra pair of hands. I'll soon get this kitchen sorted out, and I'll take over the cooking which will give Carol more time to help.'

Gerald gave her a grateful grin. 'Thanks. It was a real boost when you said you'd join us. Good chefs are like gold-dust in the Highlands!'

Which rather tactless remark made Romily wonder wryly how many they'd tried to get before they thought of asking her. But maybe she was doing them an injustice; she felt pretty sour and suspicious of everyone's behaviour towards her at the moment. Once bitten, forever shy.

After dinner, Gerald showed her round the rest of the hotel. Although this had been Carol's family home and she and Gerald had lived here for some years after their marriage, Romily had never been here before, and she was impressed by the sheer size of the place. There was a big room overlooking the lake that was to be a lounge for the guests with a smaller room opening off it as a bar. Then there was a dining-room, and a room that Gerald said had been a billiards-room was being made into a TV-cum-writing-room. 'Really somewhere where they can park the kids in the evenings,' Gerald told her. 'Not that we expect to get many children staying here—I've only advertised double rooms.'

'How many rooms?'

'We hope to have eight this year, with possibly another two in the house and three more in the converted stables, if we can run to it, next year.'

'And what about your own accommodation?'

'We're having the attic floor made into a flat with two bedrooms, a sitting-room, kitchen and bath-room. Though I'm beginning to wonder if even that will be ready on time,' he added pessimistically.

'And where have you put me?'

'In the old housekeeper's room. Through here.' He led the way to a room in one of the projecting turrets at the south-west corner of the house, looking out over the lake. To reach it you went up the main staircase to the first floor, then through a door and up a tiny little stair in the thickness of the wall to a round and quite spacious room.

'You've got your own bathroom opening off it,' Gerald told her, indicating a door in the far wall. 'But I'm afraid it's the original plumbing. We couldn't afford to have that one modernised as well at the moment.'

'Don't worry, this will do fine. Do you think you could bring my cases up now, Gerald? The drive is beginning to catch up on me.'

'Yes, of course.'

He went away and Romily looked round the room. There was a single brass bed, a wardrobe and dressing table, an old button-backed chair with frayed upholstery and a circular rug on the floor.

Not much, but the furniture had a shabby comfortableness about it that was somehow welcoming. She wondered who the housekeeper had been and whether she'd been turned out when Gerald and Carol took over. This one room would have been her home, not the whole house, just as it was about to become Romily's home.

Gerald heaved her cases in. 'Anything else you need, just shout. Carol's put soap and towels in the bathroom. Well, see you in the morning, then. Hope you sleep all right.'

'Thanks, I'm sure I will. Goodnight.'

He nodded and left. Romily gave a small sigh, kicked off her shoes, and went over to the window set into the deep thickness of the wall. It was so dark that it was impossible to see anything, but for a few minutes she just stood there, listening to the silence. After working and living in a large hotel in the heart of London it was deafening!

Her face grew grim at the thought of London. She had been so happy there at first, meeting Richard, gaining experience under master chefs, and gradually being given more responsibility. But the months had turned into years as she waited for him to commit himself, and then it had all blown up in her face and everyone had known what a fool he'd made of her.

That kind of humiliation wasn't easy to forget, even though she had tried hard to put it behind her and concentrate on her work. But it was always there, all the staff knew about it and she hadn't been able to live it down. So she'd been right to get away. But to bury herself in this Scottish backwater when she could almost have had her pick of any hotel in Europe? Romily turned back into the room and began to undress tiredly, telling herself that she didn't have to stay here for ever; she could see the hotel on its feet and then move on at the end of the summer when it closed. But the two years she had spent waiting for Richard to marry her now seemed like the most precious years of her life that had just been wasted, thrown away. She felt old, and bitter, and dried-up inside, as if she had no love and laughter left in her. Which was a hell of a way to feel when you were only twenty-five years old.

The birdsong next morning acted like an alarm clock and woke her up as the sound of heavy traffic would never have done. For a second Romily couldn't think where she was, but one look at the room brought it all back. She was at Abbot's Craig and there was a great deal of work to do. Years of living in hotels made her get up as soon as she woke and she washed quickly and put on jeans and a sweater.

But the window drew her, and this time she gave a gasp of wonder as she looked out. Watery sunshine lay across the lake and the forested hills that reached right to its shores. In the middle of the lake there was an island with what looked like a building on it, either a small house or a barn. The island seemed an interesting, mysterious sort of place and Romily wondered whether it belonged to Abbot's Craig. Perhaps fishermen used it or yachtsmen; she could see a jetty near the building. A movement on the lake caught her eye and she saw a boat, a powerboat from its speed, skimming across the grey water from the eastern side of the lake towards Abbot's Craig. For a moment she thought it must be coming there, but then she saw it go by and carry on until it was hidden by the trees

and was lost to sight. Some holidaymaker out early,
she supposed, and thought that the boat looked like
fun. But there was no time to stand and stare, she
had promised to take over the cooking and Gerald
and Carol would be wanting their breakfast.

For the next few days Romily worked really hard,
supervising the men who were installing the kitchen
equipment to the plan that she had carefully worked
out, helping Gerald to strip off old wallpaper and
put up new, painting woodwork, lining shelves for
glasses and crockery, humping furniture. Whatever
needed doing, she cheerfully lent a hand, and
gradually some sort of order began to come out of
the chaos. But it was hard work and when, on the
Saturday morning, Gerald and Carol drove into
Inverness to collect all the bed-linen they had
ordered, Romily decided to give herself some time
off.
   It was raining a little, but she longed for some
fresh air so she borrowed a pair of Carol's
wellingtons and an anorak and went out for a walk.
First she went down to the lake, finding her way to
it through the garden, down a steep flight of
overgrown stone steps to a kissing-gate, and then
along a path leading through fir trees until she came
to the water's edge. There was a small inlet below
the house with a boathouse and a wooden jetty, both
of which looked as if they had seen better days. The
boathouse had once been a fine, large building of
two storeys with stone walls and a slate roof, but
many of the slates were broken or missing now and
the rest were covered in lichen and moss, and in one
place a branch had fallen from an overhanging tree
and broken one of the windows in the upper storey.

Romily looked up at it through the misty rain, wondering if it had been used for elegant picnic parties in Victorian and Edwardian times when Abbot's Craig was in its heyday. Had the ladies sat at the big window overlooking the water, watching their menfolk while they fished from boats on the lake? For a few moments her imagination painted a romantic picture of an era in which a privileged few lived in feudal comfort, but then she thought of the other side of the coin, of the ordinary working people on whose backs the rich lived. In those days she would have been considered too young and inexperienced even to be a cook, she would probably still have been just a kitchen maid, being grudgingly taught an occasional recipe by the matriarch in charge of the kitchens! Romily laughed to herself, but wondered rather wistfully which life would have been better, one in which you knew exactly what your place was, or today's, where you rose or fell on your own merits and energy.

The rain eased as the skies began to clear. Romily shook off these rather defeatist thoughts and turned inland, not following a path or making for anywhere in particular, just walking through the trees. Drops of water fell on to her from the pines overhead and splashed into her face when she moved aside low-lying branches, but eventually the rain stopped completely, which made walking more pleasant. Often she came to fallen tree trunks which she had to climb over, and she got a little out of breath, realising that she was climbing higher all the time. The soft earth of the forest floor gave way to occasional outcrops of rock and Romily began to wonder if she ought to turn back; she didn't want to get lost. But a little further on the going became much easier, the trees grew in parallel rows instead of haphazardly and the ground had been cleared of dead wood.

She walked on, able to see the sky now through the tree branches, but presently she came to another, larger, outcrop of rock and climbed up to the top of it, where it formed a wide, deep shelf, hoping that she would be able to see where she was. Peering through the trees, Romily first looked downhill, but couldn't see the lake, then uphill and was surprised to see the battlements of a castle only about a quarter of a mile away. It must be the one she had seen from the road above Abbot's Craig on the day she had arrived. For a moment she toyed with the idea of going to have a closer look, her eyes lingering curiously on the castellated walls, but decided that she had come far enough for today and would go back. She turned to look downhill again, wondering whether to try and find the lake or to head back the way she had come. While she made up her mind, the sun came out, giving the raindrops that still clung to the pine needles a dazzling iridescence. Romily lifted her face to the warmth, wondering why on earth she hadn't got herself a job in the South of France, or somewhere equally hot, instead of this wet and inhospitable land.

'I suppose you know you're trespassing?'

The question, in a harsh, cold voice, came from behind her. Romily jumped in fright and swung round, almost missing her footing on the wet rocks. She found herself facing a tall, fair-haired man with the bluest eyes she had ever seen. The eyes had been cold, but now they widened in surprise. 'Good heavens, a girl!' He looked her over quickly, then came back to her face. 'And a pretty one at that.'

There was more than a touch of male chauvinism in that last remark, although maybe this man had more reason to be chauvinistic than most. He was well over six feet tall and proportionately broad across the shoulders. He looked like a hillman, in walking boots and waterproof clothes of a greeny-brown colour that blended with the scenery, and he carried an unloaded gun hooked over his left arm. His face, too, had the hard, clean-cut lines of the granite rocks on which he stood. All except for those blue eyes. They were the kind of eyes that you could drown in, that could make love to a woman more explicitly than any words.

Romily realised that she had been staring and her chin came up. 'I beg your pardon,' she said coldly.

'And so you should,' the stranger agreed mockingly. 'For trespassing.'

'Trespassing?' Romily looked round the forest as if it ought to be able to tell her whether she was or not. 'Is this private land, then?'

'It is,' the man assured her, his eyes on her face.

'I didn't see any signs,' she said on a slightly antagonistic note.

'There aren't any. But the land is private nearly all round the lake. Where did you come from?' he asked curiously. 'We don't get many walkers in this area.' His eyes ran over her again. 'Not that you could have come far in that get-up,' he added derisively.

Romily looked down at her wellies, slacks and anorak. 'Why? What's wrong with my clothes?' she asked in genuine surprise.

He gave a short laugh. 'It's obvious that you've never been nearer to the Highlands than a small hill! You need stout walking boots and waterproof

clothes for this terrain. You could easily slip and
break an ankle on the wet rock in those boots, and
the anorak would soon get soaked through.'

Maybe he was right, but what the hell had it got
to do with him? 'But it isn't raining,' she pointed out
acidly, and to prove her point pushed back the hood
of her anorak, at the same time stepping forward
into a patch of sunlight. Her thick auburn hair
tumbled about her shoulders, the sun turning it into
a rich swirl of molten copper.

The stranger had been about to make another
biting remark, but stopped, an arrested expression
in his blue eyes. 'Well, well, well,' he said softly.

Realising, belatedly, that she was alone with him
in the empty forest, Romily said, 'I didn't realise I
was trespassing. I'll go back.'

She turned to climb down the rocks again, but he
stepped quickly forward and said, 'No, don't go
that way. It will be easier for you to go along the
road.'

'Thanks, but I . . .'

'The road is just a short distance away, near the
castle you can see through the trees.'

Romily hesitated, then shrugged. 'All right, I'll go
that way.'

She followed him for a short way until they came
to a wide lane of grass between the fir trees, cut to
prevent the spread of forest fires, she presumed,
and here he fell into step beside her. 'You haven't
told me where you've come from,' he reminded her.

'From Abbot's Craig.'

His eyebrows rose. 'Oh yes, the new hotel,' he
said with a definite sneer in his tone. 'I didn't think
it was open yet.'

'It's not. I work there.'

'I see.' The blue eyes surveyed her with increased interest. 'And what do you do there? Let me guess, you're the receptionist?'

She smiled in amusement. So that was the impression she'd made on him; he thought she had a supposedly glamorous job. Shaking her head, she said, 'You couldn't be more wrong. I'm the cook.'

His eyes widened in surprise, but then he grinned. 'You're kidding!'

Romily shrugged and didn't answer. They had come to the end of the forest and emerged below the steep crag of rock on which the castle was built. It wasn't a vast place as castles go, but large enough, and she was glad she wasn't a poor soldier sent to besiege it. Its walls were high and thick, set on bare rock so that it seemed almost to blend with the mountainside, only its high turrets standing out against the sky. Romily gave an involuntary gasp of delight; it was a castle straight out of King Arthur, a place for knights and chivalry, for dungeons and dragons. As she looked at the windows set high, high up in the walls she almost expected a captured maiden to look out and cry for help.

'It's—breathtaking,' she said in wonderment. 'Does anyone live there now?'

'Yes. I do.'

She turned quickly to look at her companion and found him watching her with a quizzical look in his lazy blue eyes.

'You do? Do you work ...' She stopped as enlightenment came. 'No, you mean that you own it, don't you? But surely you're too young to . . .' She broke off, realising that she was becoming personal.

'Does there have to be an age limit for owning a castle?' he asked in some amusement. He lifted his head to look up at it, his eyes dwelling on the building possessively. 'It's been mine for quite some time.'

Which meant the he must either have bought or inherited it—the latter seemed most likely—at quite an early age, for he only looked to be in his mid-thirties now.

'Quite a responsibility,' Romily remarked, for something to say.

'Yes, but at least I don't turn it into a tourists' hotel with a tartan bar and haggis piped into the dining-room every evening,' he bit out harshly.

She looked at him in some astonishment, wondering what had brought that on. 'Presumably you're referring to Abbot's Craig?' she said rather stiffly.

He turned to look at her, this tall stranger who owned a castle, and his face softened. 'Sorry, but I have rather strong feelings about opening up the Highlands. Or rather *not* opening them up. And Abbot's Craig is rather near to home.'

'You want to keep it all to yourself, do you?'

Her tone had been sarcastic and a frown came into his eyes. 'I want to keep it for the people who live here all the year, not have it spoilt for them by hordes of tourists who come up here for just a week or two. The Highlands are becoming overrun by people in the summer months.' His mood changed suddenly and he grinned. 'I'm afraid you touched me on a raw spot. I don't usually start lecturing everyone I meet!' He walked with her across a lawn and round the front of the castle. 'Here's the road that will take you back to Abbot's Craig.'

'Do I have to turn off or anything?' she asked.

'No, the road only leads to here. You can't get lost.'

'Thank you, Mr . . .'

'Gordon. James Gordon.' He smiled at her, his blue eyes crinkling at the corners, and Romily's chest tightened so that she felt suddenly breathless. God, he was attractive! She nodded and turned to walk away, but he laughed and said, 'Aren't you going to tell me *your* name—or are you going to be the mystery woman in my life?'

Romily looked at him, saw his handsome face and easy smile, the slightly challenging look in his blue eyes, and there was an air of natural charm about him now despite his earlier coldness. But Romily had met that kind of easy charm before and suffered because of it. So now she answered aloofly, 'As we're unlikely ever to meet again, I'm not going to be any kind of a woman in your life, am I?'

'Oh, I don't know. After all, we'll be neighbours; we might run into one another again.'

'Hardly. Unless you come down to the hotel for a drink one evening.'

His left eyebrow rose. 'Perhaps I might do that. Would you like me to?'

It was Romily's turn to look at him mockingly. 'To a tartan bar? Why, Mr Gordon, how quickly you change your mind! No, I wouldn't dream of letting you lower your principles on my account. Goodbye. Thank you for showing me the way.' And she turned and began to walk purposefully down the road towards Abbot's Craig without giving him a backward glance.

But although she didn't look back, Romily's thoughts stayed on James Gordon as she walked along. How surprising to meet a man like that up in

the wilds of Scotland. He was the sort who would be
perfectly at home as a guest in the exclusive—and
very expensive—hotel in which she used to work.
But then he hadn't been exactly out of place in the
forest either, she remembered; he had been
confidently at ease in that environment, too. So, a
very civilised Highlander. And one who was
experienced with women. That had been obvious
from the way his eyes had assessed her, especially
after she'd taken her hood off and he'd seen her
hair. Those devastating blue eyes had become
knowing and experienced, and his manner, too, had
changed subtly, as he'd turned on the charm to
attract her. Yes, he'd been around, had Mr James
Gordon. Was he married, she wondered, or just a
playboy? She wouldn't be surprised if he was
divorced. That type usually went through several
wives, she thought cynically. Her thoughts ricochet-
ed back to Richard, the man who had told her he
loved her—only he hadn't bothered to tell her that
he already had a wife! And presumably the wife
hadn't known about her. It would have been easy
for Romily to have got her revenge by telling his
wife about their affair, but she hadn't done so; her
own hurt was bad enough, why put another
innocent person through the same kind of hell? But
somehow she didn't think that Richard's marriage
would last very long; he had already been chatting
up a new girl on the staff at the hotel less than a
month after she had found out the truth and ditched
him.

The sun went behind a cloud and it began to rain
again. Romily quickened her steps, regretting the
wide choice of places there had been in London to
go to on her days off. Rounding a bend in the road,

she saw the high walls of the castle over to her right, and wondered if she would ever see James Gordon again. It was extremely unlikely after the put-down she'd given him. Not that she thought he'd been serious about it anyway. No laird in his castle was likely to come calling on a mere cook. Especially if he had to meet her in a tartan bar! Romily chuckled to herself; she must remember to ask her brother just how he intended to decorate his bar as soon as he got home. Yes, she mused, it was rather a pity about James Gordon; he might have been worth getting to know if she wasn't so off men and if he wasn't far too macho to be taken seriously.

Gerald and Carol pulled up in the forecourt of Abbot's Craig just as Romily got back, so she was immediately co-opted into helping to unload the car and unpack all the things they had bought at the wholesale warehouse. It had done them good to get away from all the work for a while, Romily thought as she watched them; there was an air of excitement about them as they examined their new purchases, like kids after a trip to the toy shop. Gerald must have felt the same, because he said on a note of satisfaction, 'Maybe we're getting somewhere at last.' He smiled at Carol and slipped an arm round her waist, the first gesture of affection Romily had seen either of them make towards each other since she'd been there.

Tactfully, she left them alone and went into the kitchen to prepare dinner, her face tight as she remembered the way Richard used to look at her, convincing her that he loved her. And maybe he had—for a while. Oh, hell! Why did she keep thinking of Richard? She'd come up here to forget about him, hadn't she? But forgetting wasn't so easy, damn him! Her fingers tightened on the kitchen knife she was holding and she brought the point stabbing down on to the wooden chopping board in a violent blow that contained all the pent-up hurt and bitterness in her heart.

'Romily! What on earth's the matter?' Carol exclaimed in surprise as she came into the kitchen.

Opening her tightly shut eyes, Romily hastily pulled the knife out and looked in horror at the hole she had made in the board. 'Oh! Nothing. Nothing at all.' And she turned away to get some vegetables.

Carol gave her an odd look and opened her mouth to say something, but then thought better of it and put some food that she had bought into the freezer before going away again. During dinner, Gerald and Carol told her all about their shopping expedition in Inverness, and again Romily thought that they seemed much more relaxed and carefree, smiling and often laughing together.

'How did you spend your day?' Gerald asked her.

'Oh, I just went for a walk. Down to the lake and then up through the forest.'

'I should have warned you to be careful if you go into the forest. It's quite easy to get lost if you don't know the area. Sorry, I should have told you before,' her brother said, with a frown at his own forgetfulness.

'I didn't go too far. And anyway, I met someone who showed me the way to the road, so I came back that way.'

Carol was immediately interested. 'Oh, who was that? One of the rangers?'

'No. He said his name was James Gordon. It seems he owns that old castle you can see up on the hill.' She paused as Carol clumsily dropped her fork on the floor and bent to pick it up. 'I suppose you both know him from when you lived here before?' Romily added casually.

'Yes. Yes, I think we do,' Gerald answered after a moment's pause. He took a drink from his wineglass. 'Did you tell him who you were?'

'No. Should I have?'

'Oh, no, no. I just thought you might have mentioned that you were related to us, that's all.'

'No.' Romily gave a short laugh. 'As a matter of fact you don't seem to be his most popular people.'

'Why, what did he say about us?' Carol demanded sharply, her face still flushed from bending to pick up her fork.

'He didn't mention you personally, he just seemed to be very anti having this place turned into a hotel. He said the Highlands should be kept for the Highlanders and not opened up for millions of tourists to spoil.' She looked from one to the other of them. 'Do you know him well?'

'No, hardly at all,' Gerald said shortly. 'And we haven't seen him since we took over Abbot's Craig. At least I haven't.' He looked at Carol. 'Have you?'

The colour had receded from Carol's cheeks leaving her looking rather pale in comparison. 'No, I haven't.' She turned to Romily. 'This trout is really gorgeous. You must put it on the menu when we open. What have you made for pudding?'

'Another experiment for the menu. An Abbot's Craig Forest gâteau—rather like a Black Forest gâteau but with a couple of variations. Tell me what you think.'

She went to get the pudding while Carol cleared the used plates and after she'd served it they talked as before, but Romily couldn't help noticing that

Gerald and Carol had lost the sparkle they'd had
earlier; for no apparent reason the excitement had
gone and there seemed instead to be tension
between them. They didn't look at each other
directly any more and when they spoke it was as if
they were picking their words carefully.

As Romily stacked the plates in the dishwasher
after the meal, she could only guess that one of them
must have said something to upset the other while
she was out of the room getting the pudding. She
hoped it didn't mean that they were having
problems in their marriage. Because they had lived
first here and then abroad, she had seen very little of
them and had no real idea whether their marriage
was happy or not; she had just taken it for granted,
as one does, that if a couple are together they must
therefore be happy. But now that she was living
with Carol and Gerald she would be bound to get to
know them better, and just hoped that they were
happy, for the success of the hotel as much as her
own comfort. There was no way she wanted to be
dragged into any marital quarrels, or even be an
onlooker; that was something she could do without.

They went up to work on the flat they were
converting for themselves shortly after dinner, but
tonight Romily didn't offer to help, going instead to
her own room where she sat down at the desk in
front of the window to work on the menus she was
compiling. They would depend, of course, to a large
extent on what fresh produce was available, but she
wished she knew some traditional Scottish recipes
that she could use to give a flavour of the country.
Maybe she could ask Carol if her father's old
housekeeper still lived in the area, or, failing that, it
might be possible to buy an old recipe book in

Inverness, although Romily had found that it was always better to talk to an experienced cook if you could; they always had a few useful tips to hand down if you got on the right side of them.

The sound of an engine gradually getting nearer penetrated her concentration and Romily looked up. As there were no neighbours close by, she hadn't bothered to draw the curtains and although it was dark outside, the moon was out and she was high enough up to see over the trees to where its reflection turned the still surface of the lake to a rich stretch of silver. But this was suddenly broken, the surface shattering into a million rippling, dancing waves of phosphorescence as a powerful boat sped across it like a knife cutting through its tranquillity. It was the same speedboat that she had seen before, but going in the other direction now, and Romily guessed that it must belong to James Gordon; there was no other house down at that end of the lake. It slowed as it went past Abbot's Craig and she realised that the light was behind her and that he could probably see her silhouetted at the window. For a moment she felt like jumping up and drawing the curtains, but stopped herself before she'd half risen from the chair, If she did that, James Gordon would know that she was aware of him and that she was vulnerable to his arrant masculinity, and she wasn't ever going to let any man have that kind of hold over her again, she'd rather die an old maid first. So she stayed where she was, looking steadily out, until the engine was throttled into roaring life again and the boat surged on across the lake and out of sight.

CHAPTER TWO

ROMILY hardly had time to spare a thought for James Gordon over the next two busy weeks. Once or twice, when she was helping Gerald to decorate the bar—not in tartan but in a pleasant pale green wallpaper—she did remember his antipathy and wonder if he would do as he said and come down to see her; she wouldn't have been human if she hadn't thought about the incident, but he didn't phone or make any attempt to follow up the pass he'd made at her. Probably he did the same to every halfway good-looking girl he met, she thought wryly and put him out of her mind to concentrate on getting the hotel ready to open on time.

Her worries about her brother and sister-in-law's relationship happily seemed to be groundless. Admittedly, Carol started to panic because there was still so much to do, but her anxiety strangely made Gerald calmer and more capable. 'Don't worry,' he kept telling her. 'It will be all right.'

'But these guests who're coming are Americans; they expect such a high standard. And if they're not happy, they'll tell their travel agent and we'll get a bad name before we start.'

'No we won't. They'll only have to sample Romily's cooking and they won't want to leave,' her husband soothed.

'But we've got to buy lampshades for their rooms yet and I've got to collect those curtains for the TV room from the cleaners in Inverness, and I still

28

haven't finished making these cushion covers,' Carol said distractedly.

Romily exchanged a quick glance with Gerald and climbed down from the step-ladder she'd been using to hang the drapes on a half-tester bed. 'I'll go and get them for you, if you like. I wouldn't mind a look round Inverness; I haven't been there yet.'

'Oh dear, so you haven't. Yes, of course you must go. And stay and see a film or something. I'm sorry, we've been working you much too hard,' said Carol in immediate concern.

'I didn't mean that,' Romily protested, somehow feeling guilty for having said anything. 'Make a list of whatever you want in the town and I'll get everything I can.'

It would have been easy just to have changed into clean jeans and a sweater but Romily was a fashion-conscious girl and it seemed ages since she'd worn any decent clothes, so she put on a pair of leather boots and her new white coat bought for that winter, and with the main intention of impressing Richard. Romily had hardly worn it, but it was stupid just to let it hang in the cupboard because it reminded her of what might have been. Most of her clothes, anyway, she'd worn when she'd been out with Richard at some time or other. And some of them he'd even taken off her.

The day was cold but at least it wasn't raining. Romily got into her car which was still standing where she'd left it on the day she had arrived. She had some difficulty in starting the engine, but eventually it fired and she set off up the driveway and on to the road. It was one of the one-lane Highland roads which widened out into passing

places every hundred yards and you had to go along
it about three miles through heather-covered moor-
land before it reached another, larger road leading
into Inverness, about ten miles away. There were a
few other tracks leading off the narrow road, going
up to foresters' huts and one or two hill farms, but
Romily didn't pass any other vehicles as she drove
along. She skirted a big pothole in the road and had
only gone a few yards further when the car began to
pull over to one side as the steering suddenly felt
squashy under her hands.

'Oh, no, not a puncture!' Romily managed to
reach a passing place and pulled up. She was right,
the offside rear wheel was completely flat. 'Oh,
hell!' Hopefully she looked round for a farmhouse
or some other sign of habitation, but there wasn't a
house in sight. And heaven knows how far the
nearest garage is, she thought resentfully, even if
she could walk there in her high heels. And it was
nearly two miles back to the hotel, so that was out
too. She looked wryly down at her white coat. So
much for dressing up; she'd have been better off if
she'd stuck to jeans. And she was wearing an
equally good skirt underneath that she didn't intend
to ruin by changing the wheel, but it seemed that
she was going to have to if she wanted to get to
Inverness.

Thinking that if she'd been in London she would
have had half a dozen offers of help by now, Romily
opened the boot and took out the spare wheel. That
at least was OK, but she had a job to find the tools
which had somehow been left loose and found their
way down all sorts of crevices. She eventually found
them and then took off her coat, the wind
immediately striking at her and making her shiver.

With a curse, Romily hitched up her skirt and bent to loosen the wheel nuts, but they were stuck tight and she had to put an attachment on the tool and stand on it before she could get the first one loose. As she was doing so another car came round the bend behind her and stopped a few feet away.

'Don't you know you could break an ankle doing that.' James Gordon remarked as he got out of his car and strolled up to her.

Romily frowned at him. 'The nuts are jammed so tight it's the only way I can loosen them.' She became aware of his eyes travelling appreciatively up her legs and quickly stepped back on to the ground and pulled her skirt down. 'How about exerting a little masculine strength and undoing them for me? Just to save me breaking an ankle, of course.'

He gave a lazy grin. 'Well, they are extremely shapely ankles; I should hate to see one in plaster.' And he walked over to look at the wheel, then squatted down to loosen the nuts, his strong wrists having little difficulty with them. He fixed the jack in place and then looked up at her. 'Er—I take it the handbrake is on?'

Romily gave him a cool look. 'I do *know* how to change a wheel!'

With a raised eyebrow he said in mock admiration, 'You city girls, so independent! I expect you'd like to finish the job now that I've loosened the nuts for you.' And he began to straighten up.

'Oh, I wouldn't dream of depriving you of your good deed for the day. Besides, I expect it makes you feel good to come to the rescue of ladies in distress.'

James laughed. 'An answer for everything,

haven't you?' But he bent once again to change the
wheel.

Going round the other side of the car, Romily
gave a quick look to make doubly certain that she
did have the handbrake on, then wiped her hands
on a paper tissue before putting her coat on, glad to
get back into its protective warmth.

'There, that should do it.' James tightened the
last nut and stood up. 'Don't forget to get the
puncture mended as soon as you can.' He put the
wheel in the boot, then went over to his own car to
get a rag and stood looking at her as he wiped his
hands. 'Going far?'

'Into Inverness.'

'You pass a garage on the way in. They should be
able to fix it for you while you do your shopping.' He
smiled. 'You know, you still haven't told me your
name.'

'Haven't I? Sorry. It's Romily Bennion.'

His hands stilled. 'Bennion?'

'Yes, that's right.'

'The couple who own Abbot's Craig now are
called Bennion, aren't they?' he asked, his blue eyes
intent on her face.

'Yes. Gerald Bennion is my brother.'

Slowly, he began to wipe the dirt off his hands
again. 'I see. I didn't realise.' For a moment he
sounded slightly abstracted, but then he said, 'Have
you got much to do in town?'

'Quite a bit. Carol—that's my sister-in-law—has
quite a lot she wants me to get. But I was forgetting;
you know her, don't you?'

Again his eyes seemed to be fixed on her face. 'I
think we have met a few times, but it was a long
time ago. Why, did she say we knew each other?'

If she answered that truthfully Romily would have to admit that she'd talked about meeting him, but for some perverse reason she didn't feel like giving him that satisfaction, so she merely said, 'I don't believe they've ever mentioned you; I just thought that as you were next-door neighbours you were bound to have known one another.'

James gave an easy laugh. 'The two places are over a mile apart—hardly next door! And it's quite possible not to run into one another for months on end. I don't think I saw Carol's father during the last three years of his life.'

He seemed to find this perfectly natural, but to Romily it sounded distinctly odd—or anti-social. But perhaps people didn't mix very much in the Highlands. Although this particular man didn't appear to be very anti-social, in fact it was pretty obvious that he at least mixed with female company. Almost as if to prove her point, he gave her one of his devastatingly charming smiles and said, 'If you're going to be in Inverness all day, how about having lunch with me? I have some business to do this morning, but we could meet about one, if that would suit you.'

Romily hesitated, recognising a danger signal, but then gave a mental shrug. So what? She didn't know anyone else around here and one lunch couldn't do any harm. Besides, she was curious about him. But only as a person, not as a man. 'All right. Where?'

'I'd better meet you at the Tourist Information Office; you'll find it easily enough. And I'll follow you to the garage in case you have another puncture.'

'OK. Thanks.'

Romily got into her car and started off again, driving more carefully than she would normally have done if James's big car hadn't been behind her, but she reached the garage safely and turned into it, James giving her a toot on his horn as he swept by. Afterwards, she followed the detailed instructions that Carol had given and found the central car park and the shops she wanted without difficulty. Compared to London, Inverness was a doddle, there was so little of it, just one new shopping precinct and a few streets around it, and most of those seemed to contain more Highland souvenir shops than anything else.

As she did her shopping, making several trips back to the car to leave the purchases, Romily was aware of people turning to look at her, and realised that she was more smartly dressed than most of the girls she saw. But then there were only a few fashion shops in the town, nowhere near as many as there were in only one street in Central London. Although she didn't know it, Romily also drew people's eyes to her because of her tall, slim figure and attractive good looks. Whereas in London she would hardly have stood out among the thousands of good-looking girls who lived and worked there, here she rated more than a second glance from both men and women.

She had already noted the Tourist Information Office and at five to one made her way towards it. James was already there, waiting outside, on the other side of the street. He saw her almost at once and watched her as she walked with a brisk stride, her head held high and her coat swinging loosely from her shoulders. Even on this dull day her hair had the sheen of a rich new chestnut straight from the shell, and there was an aura of youth and vitality about her that made him the envy of several men who saw her go across to meet him.

He reached to take the parcel she was carrying from her. 'You didn't buy very much.'

'Oh, but I did. I took everything else back to the car.'

She fell into step beside him as he began to walk towards the High Street. 'What do you think of Inverness?' he asked her.

Romily shrugged. 'It's OK, I suppose.'

'Which means you're not impressed. I shall have to show you the castle and King Duncan's well.'

Her mind cringing at the thought, Romily said, 'Look, I've seen the Tower of London and St Paul's Cathedral, OK? That's enough to last anybody a lifetime.'

James burst into laughter, causing several people to turn round and look at them. 'You Philistine! What did you come to the Highlands for, if you don't want to see the place?'

Letting that one go, Romily quickly changed the subject. 'Where are we going to eat? Is it far?'

'No, just down that road over there.' Putting a firm hand under her elbow, James guided her across the busy High Street.

Immediately they were across Romily freed her arm and moved away from him. She had liked being treated like a piece of fragile porcelain once, but now she preferred to make her own way, even if it was only across the street.

'Here it is: the first wine-bar in the Highlands. I hope the cooking comes up to your standards.'

It was a pleasant enough place on two levels and it had the usual wine-bar arrangement of asking for

what you wanted at the counter and carrying it back
to your table yourself. The food was quite good,
though, and there was a choice of two or three hot
dishes as well as several salads. They started with
soup which was welcome after walking around in
the cold, and James ordered a bottle of wine to go
with it.

'You didn't answer my question,' James reminded her as he filled her glass. 'What brought you up to
Scotland?'

Romily frowned; she'd thought she'd ducked that
one, but she said offhandedly, 'When my brother
decided to turn Abbot's Craig into a hotel he needed
a cook, so he asked me to join them.'

'And do you have much experience?'

She gave him a cool look. 'I won't poison the
guests, if that's what you mean.'

He grinned. 'Not at all. I just wondered if this was
your first professional job as a cook.'

'No, I've worked in other places. And I *do* have
all the necessary diplomas.'

'Where did you work?'

'In London.' Romily took a sip of her wine and
deliberately changed the subject. 'I'm surprised
they don't have any traditional Scottish dishes on
the menu here. Have they all died out? Carol
doesn't know any, but then she never did much
cooking when she lived in Scotland before.'

'No, she wouldn't have. Her father kept two or
three servants.'

Romily looked at him in quick surprise; from the
way he'd spoken before it had seemed that he
hardly knew Carol's family, and yet he knew how
many staff they had employed. But he was speaking
again and the thought went out of her head. 'As for

traditional dishes, Scotland has dozens of them, everything from bannocks to Arbroath smokies.' He grinned at her look of incomprehension and explained, 'That's oatcakes and smoked haddock to you Sassenachs.'

'That's the kind of thing I want,' Romily said eagerly. 'Where can I find someone who knows all those dishes?'

'You seriously want to know?' James's left eyebrow rose slightly as if he didn't quite believe her.

'Yes, of course. The people who will be staying at the hotel will mostly be tourists; I think they'll appreciate having real Scottish dishes on the menu. Don't you?'

'I'm sure they will. Can't you get the recipes from a book?'

'I suppose so,' Romily admitted, 'but it's much better to talk to someone who's made them, if you can. You learn all the little tips that way.'

After looking down at his plate for a moment, James lifted his head and said, 'Maybe I do know someone who might be able to help you—our old cook. She's retired now and lives with her grandson in a cottage near the castle. If I asked her, she would probably talk to you, but whether she would pass on any of her culinary secrets, I don't know.'

'That's marvellous,' Romily said eagerly. 'When can I talk to her?'

He laughed. 'Tomorrow, if you like. What time are you free in the evening?'

'I could probably get away about eight.'

'All right, I'll meet you at the top of the lane leading down to Abbot's Craig at eight and take you to meet her.'

'OK. Thanks.' Romily was a little puzzled by his
not offering to come down to the house to pick her
up, but then remembered that he was so against
turning the place into a hotel. Maybe it was better
that he didn't run into Carol or Gerald in case he
couldn't resist letting them know his views and they
had a row.

They talked then of other things, of the climate,
the growth of the tourist industry and the lack of
night life for young people. And leading quite
casually it seemed from this, James said, 'I suppose
you had quite a busy social life in London, or did
you have to work every evening?'

'No, I did a sort of shift; some weeks I worked in
the evenings, others during the day.'

'So you had plenty of opportunity for dates?'

Romily picked up her glass and drank. 'Yes, I
suppose so,' she said shortly. 'Could I have some
more wine, please?'

'Of course.' James filled her glass again and she
noticed that he had good hands, long-fingered and
strong, the nails well-manicured. 'And didn't you
mind leaving all that behind? Your boyfriends, I
mean. Or don't you have a current boyfriend?'

She raised challenging eyes to meet his. 'I hardly
think you're really interested in my social life, Mr
Gordon.'

'James,' he countered her. 'And you're wrong—
I'm beginning to be very much interested in your—
social life,' he told her softly, his blue eyes taking up
the challenge and holding hers in a steady gaze.

Instinct told her to give him an immediate brush-
off, but there was something in that returned look
that made her hesitate until it was too late. Her eyes

dropped. 'No,' she said quietly, 'I don't have anyone.'

Maybe she gave something away in her tone, because he gave her a quick, assessing look, but then started talking about the local theatre. 'And there are very good theatre and concert facilities at Pitlochry,' he went on.

'Is that near here?'

'No, it's further south. You can go to a concert there and travel back the same night, but I find it more comfortable to stay overnight.' He paused. 'You will be getting a day off once the hotel gets going, won't you?'

But that was going too far too fast for Romily. Repressively, she said, 'I very much doubt it. The cooking will be entirely in my hands, so unless there's a few days when we don't have any guests I shall be working every day.'

'That sounds like slave labour. I'm sure there must be a law against anyone working seven days a week.'

Romily gave a small smile of amusement. 'Not in the hotel trade. But we're only doing breakfast and evening dinner, so I shall probably have a few hours off during the day.'

'Good, then maybe we'll be able to do this again some time.'

'Oh, but I . . .' Her hasty refusal died when she saw only casual politeness in his face and realised that she was seeing him again tomorrow anyway. 'Perhaps,' she returned offhandedly.

'When do you intend to open?'

'At Easter. We have four couples booked in for that weekend.'

'That's in less than two weeks, isn't it? Will you

be ready in time?'

'Oh, yes,' Romily answered in a completely assured tone, but with her fingers crossed under the table. 'We're just putting the finishing touches to the flat Carol and Gerald have converted for their own use.'

'They both intend to live at the hotel, do they? I mean, your brother isn't going to keep on his own job and just come up at the weekends or something?'

'No. He's given up engineering. His contract in Bahrain came to an end soon after Carol's father died, so they decided to come back to Scotland. They wanted to see more of the boys, you see.' Romily raised questioning eyebrows. 'You did know that they have two sons?'

'Yes, I think I heard. One of them was called Simon, wasn't he?'

'Yes, the younger.'

'And are the boys going to be at home with them?'

'No, they're going to stay on at their boarding-schools in England. But they'll come home for holidays, of course.'

'Yes, of course. Would you like some coffee?'

'Please.'

James went to get it and Romily watched his tall figure as he threaded his way through the tables. Was he really interested in her? she wondered. When he'd said about staying overnight at Pit-lochry, had it been a proposition or not? Usually it was easy to tell when a man was propositioning you, but with James she wasn't so sure. Maybe he'd just been sounding her out, seeing how she would react. But at least her answer had been loud and clear; she wasn't available or interested, even if she was free. Maybe it would have been better to tell him she had a boyfriend right at the start, but she didn't see why she should have to lie to protect herself. And he had at least made the suggestion in a subtle way so that it wasn't hanging between them, always in the background. That would have been unpleasant when they met in the future. If they ever met again after tomorrow. Romily remembered that he'd promised to introduce her to his old cook before he'd made that veiled suggestion. Now that she'd turned it down he might not be at all eager to see her again.

He came back with the coffee and pushed his chair out from the table to drink it so that he could cross his legs, sitting back in easy relaxation.

'Do you have a job as well as looking after your estate?' Romily asked him curiously.

He gave a short laugh. 'Are you implying by that that running an estate isn't real work?

Romily shrugged. 'I don't know. Is it? I've absolutely no idea how much—administration it involves.' She had been going to say work, but remembered his hands. They were capable hands, but they weren't the hands of someone who used them manually for a living.

'As a matter of fact it does entail quite a lot of work, but I've organised it so that it doesn't take up my whole time. And yes, I do have another job—or jobs. I'm on the boards of several firms, both in Inverness and elsewhere.'

'You're a company director, then?'

There was a hint of disparagement in her voice

which made James give her a keen glance. 'Yes,' he agreed.

He waited for her to say something to explain her tone, but Romily picked up her cup and drank the last of her coffee, evading his gaze. Richard had been a company director, although still a very junior one, in a high-powered firm that had been more important to him than anything else. Certainly more important than her and probably, she thought cynically, a great deal more important than his wife. Wherever in the world they had wanted him to go he had gone, even at only a few hours' notice. But now she came to think about it, she supposed that it was quite possible that Richard had used the firm as an excuse when he had had to break a date with her because he couldn't get away from his wife. And the opposite must certainly be true: that he'd used the firm as an excuse to get away from his wife and come to her. For a moment Romily felt physically degraded as she sat lost in bitter memories.

'They must be really unhappy ones, not worth even a penny.'

'What?' James's voice roused her from her reverie and she looked at him rather abstractedly, still hundreds of miles away.

'Your thoughts; I don't think they can be very happy ones. You looked—positively bleak.'

Romily gave a small, forced laugh. 'Did I? It was because I realised that I'd forgotten to get something for Carol that she particularly wanted. I shall be in dire trouble if I go home without it.'

'Is that all?' James didn't look as if he believed her but he let it go. 'Is Carol such a hard taskmaster, then?' he asked lightly.

'Oh, absolutely terrible! My back is covered in

lash marks from the way she whips me whenever I slow down,' Romily said facetiously.

James laughed. 'Somehow that doesn't quite ring true. From what I remember of her, Carol has far more subtle and clever ways of getting everyone to do her bidding.' He stood up. 'If you'll excuse me, I'll go and pay the bill.'

Taking the opportunity to go into the ladies' room, Romily applied fresh lipstick, then stood back to look at her reflection in the mirror. She would have to be more careful, she hadn't realised that her thoughts showed so openly on her face. Strange, though, she thought, that James had said that about Carol; he must have known the family better than he'd implied.

He was waiting for her at the entrance and they walked together back to the High Street. 'Sure you can find your way now?' James asked her.

'Oh, yes, I only have to go back to the precinct.'

'I'll leave you here, then. My car's parked at the Town Hall, in the opposite direction.'

'Goodbye, then. Thanks for lunch.'

'It was my pleasure.' He handed her parcel back to her. 'Don't forget to pick up your tyre on your way home.'

'I won't. 'Bye.' And she turned and walked briskly away from him, but this time she paused when she reached the pedestrian crossing and looked back. He was still standing on the corner, and he raised his hand in farewell as he saw her look towards him, then turned quickly and strode down the street.

'Marvellous! You've got everything I wanted,' Carol exclaimed with relieved pleasure when Romily got back. 'I'll put these curtains up straight away so that they don't crease. Can you give me a hand or are you too exhausted?'

'No, of course not. Which room are they for?'

'The television room.'

The two women carried the curtains across the hall, but it was Romily who eventually went up the step-ladder to hang them while Carol took the weight from below.

'How did you like Inverness?' Carol asked her. 'I suppose you found it very small after London.'

'You're the second person who's asked me that today. The clothes shops aren't very exciting. There's hardly any summer stuff in yet.'

'We don't often get much summery weather until well into June,' Carol reminded her wryly. 'Who was the other person?'

'What?'

'Who was the other person who asked you how you liked Inverness?'

'Oh—James Gordon. I need another curtain hook.' Romily glanced down. 'Carol, I need another hook.'

'Oh sorry.' Carol passed her one up. 'Did you run into him in town, then?'

Romily climbed down the ladder. 'There, that one looks OK. No, I had a puncture on the way and luckily he came along and changed the tyre for me. Then he asked me to have lunch with him in Inverness.'

'To have lunch?' Carol looked at her quickly and then gave a rather harsh laugh. 'I hope you said no.'

'Well, no, as a matter of fact I did have lunch with him. Shouldn't I have done?' Romily looked at the other woman in surprised puzzlement.

'Not if you value your reputation. You have to be

careful, Romily.' Carol turned to pick up the other curtain and put the hooks in. 'James Gordon is the local playboy. His intentions towards women are never—shall we say—honourable.'

'He's a womaniser, is he? I suspected as much.'

'Oh, really? Why? Did he—did he . . .'

'Make a pass? Sort of.'

'What do you mean?'

Romily looked at Carol with a slight frown but her sister-in-law's back was still towards her. 'Well, he didn't exactly come straight out and ask me to go to bed with him or anything, but he dropped a line that I could have taken up if I'd felt that way inclined.'

Carol turned to look at her, her face tight. 'But you didn't?'

'No,' Romily agreed shortly, 'I didn't.'

'Oh, good,' Carol's features relaxed and she gave a light laugh. 'I should hate to think that you'd got mixed up with our local rake before you'd been here more than a couple of weeks. I suppose I should have warned you about him. After all, I am responsible for you.'

'Thanks, but I'm quite capable of taking care of myself,' Romily answered crisply. 'And I can recognise a—a man of that type when I meet one.'

'Why—why, yes, of course. Sorry. I'm afraid I still tend to think of you as Gerald's little sister.' Carol sounded taken aback by her sharpness, but as Romily went up the ladder again, she realised that she had just told what was probably the biggest lie in her life. Richard had been a playboy, but she had been so gullible that she hadn't realised it for two years, and had only found out in the end by accident. But now, and probably for the rest of her life, she would be on her guard, and it came as no surprise to find that her suspicions about James Gordon were correct; he was far too sophisticated and good-looking to be taken seriously.

She hung the curtains and then climbed down. 'They look good, don't they? Match the wallpaper perfectly.'

'It's the other way round; I chose the paper to go with the curtains. Of course we could really do with a new carpet in here, but it will have to wait until we've got some money coming in, I'm afraid,' Carol answered, looking round the room. She paused, then added, 'I really do feel that it would be better if you didn't see James again. He's good-looking, of course, but not the type a girl wants to get—well, involved with, if you see what I mean.'

'You don't have to worry, I'll keep him at a distance.'

'You haven't—you haven't arranged to meet him again, have you?' asked Carol with some alarm in her voice.

Romily didn't particularly want to discuss her private life with Carol, but realised that in a place like this it would probably get back to her anyway, so admitted reluctantly, 'Yes, tomorrow night, as a matter of fact. But only because he's going to introduce me to his old cook. I want to see if I can learn some old Scottish dishes from her.'

'Oh, I see. Well, be careful, won't you? I know he's very attractive to women, but he isn't any good for you, my dear.'

'I'll remember,' Romily said lightly. 'Is there anything else you want me to help you with, or shall I go and decide what to make for dinner?'

Alone in her kitchen, Romily got down a couple

of cookery books and began to go through them, but her mind drifted back to that conversation with Carol. She wondered how her sister-in-law had known that James was a womaniser when she'd lived abroad for such a long time, but then realised that she probably still had a great many friends in the area that would have brought her up to date on all the latest gossip. Or Carol might be basing her warning on the fact that James had that kind of reputation before she went to Bahrain. Fleetingly Romily wondered if perhaps James might have changed and grown out of his libertine tendencies in the ten years that Carol had been away, but then dismissed the idea. Once a stud, always a stud, she decided with bitter cynicism. She was glad that Carol had warned her against him; now she would be doubly on her guard.

And it was with this thought in mind that she walked up the lane to meet James the following evening. It was dark, the moon not yet out, and she carried a torch to light her way. The night was dry, but there was a cold wind so she had put on a thick coat and tied a scarf, gypsy-fashion, around her hair. Romily had expected to see a car parked at the end of the lane and stopped to look round for it.

'Hallo, Romily.'

She turned quickly, surprised to see James standing nearby. 'Where's your car?'

'I thought we might walk up. Do you mind?'

'No, I suppose not.' She lifted her torch to see him better. He was bareheaded, but was wearing a thick Aran sweater under his jacket.

He smiled. 'Good. I was afraid you might be wearing four-inch heels or something.' She fell into step beside him, just able to make out his figure in the darkness. 'I don't suppose you did much walking in London,' he remarked.

'On the contrary. I like to walk. I often used to go into Hyde Park, and sometimes we went jogging on Hampstead Heath.'

'We?'

'A—some friends and I,' Romily prevaricated.

'There are some good walks round here, but it's advisable to go with someone who knows the area. It's easy to get lost, and sometimes the mist can come down quite suddenly.'

'I should have thought you'd get more climbers than walkers,' she remarked.

'We get some. The Monadhliath mountains just south of Inverness are quite high and they lead down to Ben Nevis, but most people who come to climb them stay at Fort William or Fort Augustus.'

'You're glad to say,' she observed with mock wryness.

James laughed. 'The walkers and the climbers I can understand; at least they get to know the countryside and have a respect for it. It's the hundreds of tourists in their coaches and caravans I can't tolerate. All they ever seem to do is to drive from one whisky distillery to another, and from town to town where they make for the nearest souvenir shops. If they ever walk more than half a mile from their car or coach I should be very surprised.'

'But think of all the work they bring to the area.'

'And think of all the unemployment they leave behind in the winter. It's no real solution to the problem.' He glanced at her. 'Does Abbot's Craig intend to stay open in the winter?'

'I don't think so. Gerald said he would probably

close at the end of October, but he's thinking of opening again for the New Year if he can get enough bookings.'

'And what will you do in the winter?'

Romily shrugged. 'I haven't thought about it. Get a job somewhere hot, I should think,' she said with a shiver.

'It does warm up a bit in the summer.'

'But not much?'

'We have been known to have heatwaves, but they are, I must admit, something of a rarity. Are you very cold?'

Afraid that he might offer to keep her warm, Romily said, 'No, I'm fine. What's your cook's name?'

'Mrs MacPherson. I've always called her Maggie, but she can be a bit of a martinet, so I think you'd better stick to being formal for a start.'

'Why? Does she disapprove of the younger generation?'

'Not really. But she's a bit wary of strangers at first.'

'And especially English and female strangers, I suppose.'

James grinned. 'I'm sure you'll twist her round your little finger.'

'I doubt it. I'm not you.'

'What makes you think I can?'

'Oh, I'm quite sure you're extremely good at twisting women round your little finger,' Romily retorted, unable to keep an acid note out of her voice.

If he'd heard, he gave no sign of it. 'Maggie is a special case,' he told her. 'I've known her all my life. She used to let me have midnight feasts that no one else knew about, when I was a boy.'

'You mean she spoiled you rotten.'

'Something like that,' he agreed with a laugh. 'And when your brother's two boys are home and sneak into the kitchen looking for something extra to eat, won't *you* spoil them rotten?'

'Why, yes, I suppose I will,' Romily admitted, rather liking the mental picture this brought to her mind. 'But I expect they're used to midnight feasts at school.'

'They'll still try to steal cakes and biscuits if they can. Boys can never get enough of those.' James flashed the powerful torch he was carrying off to the right. 'We go up here.'

Romily saw that they were almost at the castle and that there was a track going off below it. It was wide enough to take a car, so they continued to walk along side by side. She was aware of tall trees either side of them and once some creature in the forest gave a piercing cry quite nearby, startling her so that she turned in swift alarm. 'What was that?'

'It's all right,' James reassured her, 'It's only an owl. We must have startled it.'

'Not half as much as it startled me! I suppose there are quite a lot of animals roaming about in the woods at night,' she said rather nervously.

'Yes, but none that aren't more frightened of you than you are of them.'

Romily rather doubted that but let it go. Ahead of them she saw a light and they soon came up to a stone-built cottage. James rapped on the door and it was opened by a small, sprightly looking woman of about seventy.

'Hello, Maggie,' James greeted her. 'Here's the young lady I was telling you about.'

Maggie gave Romily a good long look before she said, 'Come you in, then.'

As she stepped into the hall, Romily said, 'Good evening, Mrs MacPherson. It's very kind of you to let me come and talk to you.'

'We'll go into the parlour,' Maggie said decisively, showing them into a small but very clean room where a young man was reading the paper in front of a brightly burning fire. He jumped to his feet as they came in and Maggie introduced him as, 'My grandson, Ian.'

Ian looked to be about her own age, possibly a bit younger, and he obviously hadn't expected anyone at all like Romily. He stammered a little as he greeted her and wiped his hand on his jeans before he offered it to her. Maggie gave him an impatient look and asked them to sit down, her eyes again going over Romily in the better light.

It was warm in the room, so Romily unbuttoned her coat, but she didn't like to take it off when Maggie hadn't asked her to. She felt very much that she was on trial and that if she said or did anything wrong, Maggie would never take her into her confidence and part with any of her culinary secrets. James, though, was completely at home and started talking to both Maggie and Ian about ordinary, everyday things while Romily sat quietly by, but gradually and cleverly he brought her into the conversation so that they were all four talking together. Then James subtly switched to talking about forestry work to Ian, leaving the two women to hold a separate conversation. Following his tacit lead, Romily didn't attempt to ask Maggie directly to help her, instead encouraging her to talk of the years when she had been the cook up at the castle.

The old lady reminisced for about half an hour and then got to her feet. 'Maybe you'd like to try one of my oatcakes? And won't you take off your coat, now?'

'Thank you, I'd very much like to try one.'

Maggie went out and returned with a tray of hot oatcakes which she spread with butter, inviting them to help themselves to jam or honey. She watched as Romily bit into hers, waiting for her judgement. The oatcake was delicious, and Romily told Maggie so, but was careful not to overdo it. 'You cook them on a griddle, don't you?' she asked.

'Aye, we do. We call them bannocks.' She paused for a minute, then seemed to come to a decision and nodded her head. 'Come you into the kitchen and I'll show you.'

So they left the two men and Romily was given her first lesson in Scottish cooking. It was a dish that she could have made quite easily by herself from a recipe, but she realised that she would have to go at Maggie's pace and serve a kind of apprenticeship before the old lady would teach her about any less common dishes. Maggie's grey eyes watched her keenly as she worked and occasionally nodded with satisfaction. 'Aye, you'll do,' she remarked when the bannocks were finished. 'You've a light hand.'

'And maybe if she has enough practice she might be as good as you in twenty years or so. Isn't that what you're thinking, Maggie?' James came into the kitchen and slipped an arm round Maggie's waist. 'Am I going to be allowed to try one?'

'Off with you! I'll not have a man cluttering up my kitchen,' Maggie scolded him. But it was obvious that she loved every minute of his teasing despite what she said, and James soon got an oatcake to try.

'Mm,' he said, 'I'd say at least ten years before they're as good as yours. What do you think, Ian?'

But Ian wasn't so tactful. 'They taste just as good to me,' he said approvingly.

James shot him a quick glance and adroitly changed the subject, but Maggie was starting to look a little tired so he soon said, 'I shall expect you to send some of these bannocks up to the castle tomorrow, Maggie. You've been neglecting me lately. And now I must take Romily home.'

'No need for you to go all the way back there, Mr Gordon,' Ian put in. 'I can walk the young lady back to Abbot's Craig.'

Romily looked at him in some surprise. Ian had hardly spoken to her directly more than a couple of times all evening, and as he had a broad accent she had sometimes found it a little difficult to understand him, although she could understand Maggie's attractive Scots burr perfectly well. But it seemed that she had made more of an impression on him than he had on her. He was stockily built and a few inches taller then Romily, although he seemed short in comparison to James, and he was presentable enough with thick brown curly hair that had a touch of red in it and a pleasant, open face.

There was a determined look about his face now, but James easily took matters into his own hands, 'I wouldn't dream of tearing you from your fireside.' Picking up Romily's coat, he helped her into it. 'Goodnight to you both. Thank you, Maggie.'

'Goodnight, Mrs MacPherson,' Romily echoed. 'When we put bannocks on the menu at the hotel I shall call them Maggie MacPherson's bannock cakes.'

The old lady gave a merry laugh, much pleased. 'When you have a free afternoon you can come up and I'll teach you how to make real Scots porridge.'

'Thank you, I'll certainly do that. Goodnight, Ian.'

Their hosts watched them a little way down the road before shutting their door. Romily turned to wave and stumbled a little, her eyes not yet used to the darkness. James caught her arm to steady her and didn't take away his hand. 'All right?'

'Yes, thanks.' He had switched on his torch and Romily fumbled in her pocket for her own, but couldn't find it. 'Oh, darn!' She came to a stop.

'What is it?'

'I left my torch behind. I'd better go back for it.'

'Don't bother; mine's powerful enough. I'll collect yours for you tomorrow and drop it in to you.'

Romily hesitated, but the moon had come out and the night was lighter now.

'Come on,' urged James, and she automatically began to walk along with him. She drew her arm away from his hold but found that when the moon went behind a cloud and there was only the one torch she had to stay quite close beside him anyway.

They didn't hurry, it was only about ten o'clock and it wasn't unpleasant out in the crisp clean air.

'I told you you'd twist Maggie round your little finger,' James remarked. 'And it seems as if you've made a conquest of Ian too. But it might be better not to get too friendly with him; he's the strong, silent type who takes everything very seriously.'

Romily laughed, thinking how Carol had warned

her off James for the very opposite reason.

'Why do you laugh?'

'It doesn't matter.'

'Tell me,' he commanded, his footsteps slowing.

'No. It's nothing.' She tried to walk on, but he stayed still and she couldn't see enough without the torch.

'Do you like boating?' he asked unexpectedly.

'Boating? You mean sailing?'

'No, motor-boating.'

'I don't know, I've never been on one.'

'If the weather's fine on Sunday how about coming out with me on mine? We can go up the Caledonian Canal to Inverness and out into the open sea.'

Romily remembered the speedboat she had seen on the lake and felt a thrill of excitement at the thought of going out in it, to slice through the waves and have the wind in her hair. She loved speed but so far had only ever experienced it in a car with Richard . . . Her thoughts came to an abrupt stop and she turned to walk on. 'I don't think so, thanks,' she said shortly.

His tone mocking, James caught her up and said, 'Afraid of being seasick?'

'No.'

'What, then?'

'I just don't think it would be a very good idea.'

'All right, we'll go for a walk instead.'

They had come to the top of the driveway leading to Abbot's Craig and Romily stopped. 'I can find my own way from here. Thanks for taking me . . .'

'No, you can't,' James interrupted. 'If the moon goes in you'll probably fall over and break something.' Before she could protest any further he began to walk down the driveway. 'You haven't answered me,' he reminded her. 'Will you come out walking on Sunday?'

'No. Sorry.'

'Are you?' he said rather cynically.

'Am I what?'

'Are you sorry? Or are you trying to tell me to get lost?'

'Why should I want to do that?' she prevaricated.

'I don't know. We got on fine together yesterday, but tonight you seem different—tense, more withdrawn.'

'I was probably nervous of meeting Mrs Mac-Pherson.'

'No, you weren't.' They had come to the big, open archway leading to the inner courtyard and James came to a stop. He turned off the torch and put it on the ground, but the moon was bright now and there was enough light for her to see his face. 'What is it, Romily? What's the matter?'

'Nothing. I'm no different.'

'Then come out with me on Sunday.' Reaching out, he took hold of her waist and drew her towards him.

Romily gave a little gasp as she realised what he was going to do and said hastily, 'No. No, I don't want you to.'

She put a hand against his shoulder, but he easily pulled her against him. 'Don't be silly,' he said huskily, and bent to kiss her.

She tried to push him away, but his arm was like a steel belt round her waist, holding her close to him, and when she tried to turn away he put his hand behind her head and held her prisoner beneath his mouth. For a moment she was angry and tried to

resist him, but her ego as much as her heart had
been battered when she'd found out the truth about
Richard, and it was strangely comforting to be
desired again. That need for comfort and reassur-
ance made her relax her defences a little, and it was
then that his kiss got to her, insinuatingly reaching
deep into her feminine sensuousness, making her
aware of herself as a woman again, making her
remember what it was like to be held in a man's
arms, to be kissed and touched and loved.

Suddenly she pushed him fiercely away. 'Damn
you, I said no!' Angrily she stepped back from him
but was brought up short by the wall. 'Keep away
from me!'

James stood very still for a moment, then said
evenly, 'All right. But you'd better say no with more
conviction next time.'

'There won't be a next time!'

'I see. Are you going to tell me what I've done to
upset you?' She didn't answer and he went on, 'Or
maybe it's because you've been warned to stay away
from me, is that it?'

'That shouldn't surprise you,' Romily answered
coldly.

'It doesn't. There's no love lost between your
brother and me.'

'Oh, but it wasn't . . .' Romily began in surprise,
then stopped in confusion.

'So it was Carol, was it? I suppose I should have
guessed.' James made an angry gesture with his
hand. 'Why the hell couldn't she let well alone?'
Taking a step towards her, he said earnestly, 'Look,
Romily, I don't know what or how much Carol has
told you, but I assure you that it has nothing to do
with us. As far as I'm concerned the past is over and

done with. I know it's early days and we've only just
met, but I would really like us to get to know each
other better. If you've heard stories about me, then
I'm sorry, but there's nothing I can do about that—
except ask you to take me as I am, to judge me on
how I behave to you.'

Romily laughed harshly. 'You just kissed me
against my will,' she pointed out.

'No, not against your will,' James demurred, his
voice softening. 'And it was only a kiss goodnight;
where's the harm in that?' Lifting a hand, he gently
touched her cheek, his fingers warm against her
cold skin. 'And you're not a naïve young girl,
Romily; you've been kissed goodnight before.'

Her face whitened and she tossed her head away
from his hand. 'That doesn't give you the right to—
handle me!'

James's mouth twisted in amusement. 'Hardly.
But it does mean that we're both civilised people.
We ought to be able to accept a person for what he
is, without prejudging. And as for that kiss—well,
kisses are very pleasant things to exchange, but they
don't commit you to anything. They're just a sign of
warmth, and friendship, and an acknowlededgment
that I'm a man and you're a woman, and that I find
you very attractive.' He was on dangerous ground
again and Romily opened her mouth to speak, but
he said quickly, 'But that's as far as it goes. So, on
those terms, in friendship and getting to know one
another better, will you come out with me on
Sunday?'

His tone was ingenuous, his smile charming and
persuasive, but Romily had been taken in by
persuasive charm before. 'No,' she said clearly, 'I
think it would be much better if we didn't see one

another again. Goodnight.' And she turned quickly away and ran through the archway towards the lights of the house.

CHAPTER THREE

ALL next day Romily waited in a little trepidation for James to arrive with her torch. After the way she'd walked out on him last night she expected him to be annoyed with her at least, and imagined that he would treat her with cold antagonism, an attitude that she thought he would be rather good at. It wouldn't be pleasant, but it didn't worry her unduly. There was no way she wanted to get to know any man other than as a friend or acquaintance right now, but James obviously wanted more than that, and as she wasn't prepared to give it their relationship might as well end now as later. But she was also afraid that James might come to the hotel and be seen by Carol, who would immediately want to know why she hadn't taken her advice and start asking all sorts of questions. As it was, her sister-in-law had already tried to find out what had happened last night at Maggie's, but Romily had merely told her that she'd been given a lesson in making bannocks and then deliberately talked about something else.

But as it turned out, it wasn't James but Ian who brought her torch back. He turned up at five o'clock, running into Romily when she was standing in the driveway cutting back some overgrown bushes and where she had intended to intercept James before he reached the house.

'I've brought your torch back for ye,' he told her.

'Oh, thanks.' Romily put down the saw she was

using to take it from him. 'Er—did Mr Gordon ask you to bring it down?'

'No. I saw it this morning and put it in my pocket, but I've no had a chance to bring it afore.'

'Oh, I see. Well, it's very kind of you. Thank you.'

She expected him to go, but he just stood there so Romily turned back to her task, wanting to finish the job before the light went.

'Yon garden needs a lot of work,' Ian observed. 'Do ye no have a man to do it?'

'No, but my brother hopes to have some time to spend on it once the house is finished. You know it's being turned into a hotel, don't you?'

'Aye, the laird told us.'

For a moment Romily was puzzled, but then realised that James must be the local laird, or lord of the manor.

'When will you be coming to the house for another cookery lesson?' Ian asked.

Guessing that he would make a point of being there when she did, Romily prevaricated, saying, 'I'm not really sure. It depends when I can get away.'

'Romily dear, you really mustn't overwork yourself, you know. I . . .' Carol came round the bend in the drive and stopped in surprise when she saw Ian. 'Oh, sorry, I didn't realise you had someone with you.' She smiled at Ian. 'Hallo.'

Which was a lie, Romily thought. Carol must have heard their voices, but her surprise had been genuine enough. So who had she been expecting to see? James, perhaps? Romily didn't like being checked up on even if Carol did have the best of intentions, and she was certainly too old to have anyone watching over her, so she said rather coldly,

'This is Ian MacPherson. It was his grandmother
who taught me to make the bannocks.'

'Ian MacPherson! Good heavens.' Carol gave a
delighted laugh. 'Of course it is. But you've changed
so much in the last ten years I didn't recognise you.
But then you were only about thirteen or fourteen
when we left, weren't you?'

She held out her hand and Ian shook it after
wiping his on his trousers, and the two talked
together while Romily got on with her job. Then Ian
said, 'Could I talk to you for a minute, Mrs
Bennion?'

'Yes, of course. Come in and have a cup of tea.
Are you coming, Romily, or do you want to go on?'

So much for worrying that I'm overworking,
Romily thought grimly, her suspicions confirmed.
'No, I'll clear up here first.'

She half expected Ian would offer to help her but
he followed Carol round to the back of the house. It
took a while to clear up the cuttings and take them
in the wheelbarrow to the rubbish pile and it was
nearly dark when Romily went back indoors. 'Has
Ian gone?' she asked Carol, as she took her coat off
in the kitchen.

'Yes. Isn't it marvellous—he offered to come and
work on the garden here in his spare time. We're
paying him, of course, but he didn't want very
much, thank goodness. The thought of the garden
was really beginning to worry me. And it's a load off
Gerald's mind, too. He never did like gardening
very much.'

'Whose idea was it, yours or Ian's?'

'I told you, his. I suppose he could do with the
extra money.'

For what, Romily wondered. So that he could

save up and leave home? Or had he made the offer so that he would have the opportunity of seeing more of her? She had, she knew made quite an impression on him last night, but the last thing she wanted was for Ian to follow it up, especially if what James had said was true and Ian was the serious type. To her, Ian was only a boy, and she didn't want to hurt him. Neither did she want any complications in her life. She sighed, hoping that she was worrying over nothing and that Ian really was interested only in making some extra money.

He arrived to work in the garden for the first time two days later on the Saturday afternoon, but Romily very adroitly foiled any plans he might have had by going up to his grandmother's cottage to learn how to make real Scots porridge.

Mrs MacPherson greeted her with a pleased smile. 'I'm on my own again this afternoon, so I'm glad to see you.' They started on the porridge, using fresh oatmeal, and today Maggie was far more talkative and forthcoming. 'You must always stir the porridge with your right hand, clockwise,' she instructed.

'Why?' Romily asked in puzzlement.

'Because that's the way it's always been done,' Maggie told her, as if this was explanation enough. 'And you must always use a straight wooden stick like this. It's called a spurtle. And you serve it with *cold* milk, not hot like they do below the Border. And sugar if you must, but it's much better with salt. True Scotsmen always used to eat it standing up, you know. It was the custom.'

She was a mine of memories and traditions and it was fun to listen to her and learn from her, but when Romily asked about other Scottish dishes she shook her head. 'One recipe a day is quite enough.'

Crafty old woman, Romily thought with a smile as she left; now she's sure of me spending an afternoon with her at least another dozen times. Not that Romily minded, she had enjoyed today, but it was nice to get out in the fresh air again after the heat of Maggie's kitchen. It had been raining yesterday, but now it was dry and windy, yet the wind wasn't so cold and you could almost feel the first hint of spring coming from the south. Romily didn't know what time Ian would be working till, but she didn't particularly want to run into him, so instead of going back to Abbot's Craig by the road she cut through the trees below the castle and kept going downhill until she reached the lake. If James had a boat, then he probably had a boathouse and a proper path leading down to it, but Romily had no wish to meet James either, so she went down through the trees. She had seen nothing at all of him since he had taken her to Maggie's and guessed that she had injured his masculine pride and that he would leave her severely alone in future, but she judged that it would still be best to keep out of his way.

Romily reached the lake and walked along beside it, lifting her head to the breeze. She loved to feel the wind in her hair; in London it was always full of dust and dirt but here the air was clean and smelt of the tall Scots pines that adorned the hillsides. She stopped to look at some tiny yellow celandines that were just beginning to appear in a sheltered spot beneath the trees, marvelling that they had survived the snow of winter. After walking on for another half-mile, Romily came to the tumbledown boathouse below Abbot's Craig. From here she could see that the island in the lake lay midway between the hotel and the castle, and she wondered who owned it. The picture it made, with the house half hidden among the trees, caught at her imagination and she rather gingerly walked on to the jetty that stuck several yards out into the water to get a better view. There had been a handrail once, but this had mostly broken away and she didn't attempt to use what was left; the planks were about two yards wide and looked solid enough, although they were rather slippery where moss and algae had started to grow on them.

From here she could see the island a little better and realised that the house was quite small, stone-built and about the size of Maggie's cottage. There was no smoke coming from the chimney, though, and it looked unlived-in, which seemed a shame; it would make—at the least—a very pleasant holiday cottage. She must ask Gerald about it; even if it didn't belong to him it might be an idea to rent it and do it up. It would make a good added attraction for the hotel. She stood for a little longer, silhouetted against the open expanse of the lake, and had just turned to go in when she heard the sound of a boat coming fast towards her and lifted her head to see the now familiar hull of James's boat surging through the water. There was no time to run to the trees; it was impossible for him not to have seen her, just as it was impossible for her not to have heard the sound of that powerful engine, so Romily stayed where she was, hoping that he would go straight past.

It was a forlorn hope. James slowed the engine and brought the boat to a neat stop just at the end of the jetty, holding it there with the engine idling quietly, like a purring leopard taking a rest but ready to burst into snarling life again at any moment.

'Whenever I see you,' James commented, 'you're doing something dangerous! Have you got a death-wish or something? Or are you just accident-prone?'

'But I haven't had an accident,' Romily pointed out, unable to repress a slight grin at this.

'In that case you must lead a charmed life.' He put a hand out to hold the tall wooden post at the end of the jetty, pulling the boat closer in. 'Am I forgiven yet for the other night?' he asked her, his blue eyes searching her face.

Romily knew full well what he meant, but chose not to show it. 'Forgiven?'

'For kissing you against your will,' he told her, making it sound dramatic.

Carefully she answered, 'One should only ask for forgiveness if one is sorry for what one has done.'

James pretended to look crestfallen. 'Oh dear, in that case I may never be forgiven, because I'm not in the least sorry. I enjoyed every, all-too-short, minute of it.' Then he grinned at her. 'Are you always this pompous?'

'Pompous!'

Putting on a po-face, he mimicked, 'One must be sorry for what one has done.'

Romily couldn't resist laughing. 'Oh dear, was it as bad as that?'

'Much worse. But seeing you laugh is much, much better. Am I forgiven, then?' he asked again with a smile.

His smile was as irresistible as his teasing and Romily only hesitated for a second before saying with a shrug, 'I suppose so.'

'Good. Then come for a ride with me.'

'You—you mean now?'

'Yes, of course.'

'But—but it's getting dark.'

'Just round the lake,' he tempted. 'So that you can see what it's like.'

Romily glanced across at the island that she found so mysterious and intriguing. Putting on a Cockney accent, she aped the men who ran seaside boat trips and said, 'Just once round the island, guv'nor?'

James gave a delighted grin and immediately joined in the game. 'That's right, me ducks. Step aboard the *Skylark!*' He held out his free hand to her, which Romily took and jumped lightly on board, sitting next to him in the front seat.

'Hold on!' he shouted as the engine roared into life, and then they were dashing across the still lake, the prow of the boat high out of the water as the powerful outboard thrust them along. The wind tore at them, making Romily's hair whip round her head like Medusa's coils. She clung to the handrail, loving every second, and lifted large, exhilarated eyes to James. 'Can't you go any faster?' she yelled.

He gave a shout of laughter and opened the throttle even wider, sending the boat surging across the surface of the water faster than the wind. They went round the lake in minutes, but James kept on going for a second time. The speed thrilled her, filling her with exultation, and she stood up the better to feel the wind on her face, but James pulled her back into her seat and slowed down. She turned a disappointed face towards him. 'Why have you stopped?'

He laughed. 'We can't keep going round in

circles. Come with me tomorrow to the open sea and I'll show you what she can really do.'

'All right.' The words were out before Romily had time to even think about them.

'Great. I'd better take you back now, it's getting quite dark.'

'No, wait.' They were opposite the island now and she could see the house much closer. 'Does anyone live there, in that house?'

'No. No, it's empty.'

He leaned forward to reach for the throttle but she put a hand on his arm. 'It looks so mysterious. Who owns the island?'

'I do.'

'Do you?' She turned to look at him. 'I—I'd love to go there some time,' she said after hesitating because he might take it suggestively.

But to her surprise he was dismissive. 'There's nothing much to see. The house hasn't been lived in for years and is probably riddled with damp. I'm thinking of having it pulled down. Now I must get you back before it gets too dark for you to find your way home. Did you get your torch, by the way?'

'Yes, Ian brought it.'

James grinned. 'I heard he'd stolen a march on me. But I hope that's all he stole,' he added softly.

Romily didn't know how to take that, so didn't answer. They sailed to the old jetty, slowly this time, and James tied up the boat before stepping on to it and helping her after him. Then he insisted on walking with her as far as the kissing-gate at the bottom of Abbot's Craig's garden. 'You'll be all right from here, won't you?'

'Yes, of course.' She went through the gate and stood on the other side.

'What time shall I pick you up tomorrow?' he asked.

'Oh. Oh yes, tomorrow. Will—will ten-thirty be all right?'

'Fine. I'll meet you here, then, shall I?'

'OK. Goodnight.'

'Goodnight.' James caught her hand. 'You know,' he said ruefully, 'this is an awful waste of a kissing-gate. But I don't want to make you run away from me again, so . . .' he lifted his hand in farewell, 'until tomorrow.'

Her acceptance of his offer had come when she was exhilarated from the boat ride, but as the adrenalin went out of her brain so doubts began to creep in. She had decided not to have anything more to do with James, and yet here she was fixing up to go out with him the next day. And what would Carol have to say to that? Nothing, if she didn't tell her, was Romily's immediate reaction, years of living among people she worked with having taught her to keep her private affairs to herself. Only at the last hotel she'd been working in she hadn't been able to. Everyone had known that she and Richard were in love because Richard had let everyone know it—always asking for her the minute he checked in, sending flowers down to the kitchens for her, and insisting on her having a drink with him at the bar. At first the staff manager had disapproved; they didn't like the staff mixing with the guests, but somehow Richard had talked him round and it had gone on for so long that in the end everyone had just taken it as a matter of course. Which was why it had been all the more disastrous when it had all blown up in her face.

Now, Romily determined to keep her outing with

James a secret from her brother and sister-in-law, if
she could. Not only did she not want to upset them,
but she didn't want to have to live in a strained
atmosphere if they made their disapproval known.
After all, they had been living abroad for so long
that they had forfeited any right they might have
had to govern her life. Even if she hadn't done it
with any notable success, she had at least been her
own mistress for several years now. And Richard's
mistress too, of course, she thought with fierce
bitterness. Only it hadn't seemed as sordid as that at
the time. She had been hopelessly in love with him
and he had used every persuasion to make her agree
to let him make love to her, but it was only when he
had talked of marriage and their future together
with such certainty that she had at last given in.
And all the time he had been lying in his teeth.

Romily tried hard to push the bitterness out of
her mind while she cooked dinner, but she felt low
and depressed all evening. Luckily Carol and
Gerald were going out that night to a christening
party for a friend's child. Romily had been invited
to go with them, but she said she'd rather not and
instead sat in front of the TV set while she dried her
hair, Before, her life had seemed so full; when
Richard was in town he had taken her out
somewhere every night, usually to jazz clubs—he
was mad keen on jazz. And at the other times, when
he was back in his home town of Manchester, there
had always been other girls on the staff of the hotel
to go out with, or sometimes they had gone out in a
crowd with some of the waiters and young trainee
chefs. But life had always been lived at a fast,
exciting pace. Now her social life seemed to have
come to a standstill, like an express train that had

slammed on its emergency brakes. From the moment she'd found out about Richard, almost three months ago now, Romily had shut herself away and not gone out at all, except for solitary walks in a park. But this evening, for the first time since that dreadful day, when she had gone out in James's boat she had felt exhilarated and excited again, young and alive.

But to come back to the lonely present after the exhilaration somehow seemed to make it worse, and Romily felt more depressed than she had since she'd arrived at Abbot's Craig. She almost wished that she had gone with Carol and Gerald, but then dismissed the idea; she would have been completely out of place with all the married couples. Better to be on her own, and there was always tomorrow to look forward to when she would be out on the boat again. And James, was she looking forward to seeing him again, too? Going out with him for a second time could be taken as giving him some encouragement. She would have to be careful if his reputation was a true one. And he certainly hadn't denied it, had even seemed to take it for granted that Carol and Gerald knew all about him. With a reputation like that James was the last person she should be going out with, but Romily had to admit that there was something about him that was madly attractive, not just his looks or his size, but some sort of basic magnetism that emanated from his supreme self-assurance and an inborn positiveness of manner. And added to this, he had a touch of arrogance and a slight cynicism that couldn't fail to catch and hold a woman's attention.

With a personality like that, he must have had loads of women. So why was he interested in her?

Romily wondered. OK, she was vain enough to know that she was more than pretty, but even so ... Maybe it was just because she was new on the scene and he made a point of trying to make it with every girl who came his way. Which was a pretty sick thought. Getting up, Romily turned off the TV set with a snap, fed up with watching a film that she thought would be a thriller and turned out to be a love story. Men were all the same, all they ever wanted from you was sex. No matter how they dressed it up and made it appear romantic, it all boiled down to the same thing in the end. But she had been used by a man once and would make darned sure she never would be again. It would be the other way round, she decided fiercely. She would use James Gordon. As a provider of exciting boat rides, as an escort when she needed one, and as a means of relieving the boredom of the Highlands. And if he thought he was going to get any sexual rewards from her for that, well—he could just go to hell with every other man in the world like him!

CHAPTER FOUR

ROMILY read in bed until about one in the morning, but Carol and Gerald still hadn't arrived home when she turned off her light and went to sleep. The next morning a heavy mist lay in the valley and the air felt damp, so she put on jeans, a shirt and a thick sweater before going down to make herself some breakfast. Carol's evening bag and jacket were on the floor in the hall, so Romily picked them up and put them on the table with a smile; evidently they had had a good time at the party. She moved around quietly, not wanting to wake them, although there was little chance of that when they were two floors above her. Today Gerald didn't even come down to get the morning paper and take it back to bed with him with a cup of tea, as he usually did on Sunday mornings, so Romily had it all to herself.

At about nine-thirty the mist began to clear and at ten-twenty, when she put on her boots and let herself out of the house, a weak sunshine had begun to break through and it promised to be a fine morning. She walked slowly down through the garden, seeing where Ian's work had already made an impression on the overgrown hedges. She wondered if Gerald would get him to mend the jetty and whether he would buy a boat for the use of any fishermen that came to stay at the hotel. It might be fun to have a boat, although it wouldn't be anywhere near as powerful as James's, of course. Still, she might be able to go over and explore the island in it.

From where she was standing on the lower lawn, Romily saw the speedboat appear round the bend below the castle. It was travelling quite slowly, not making enough noise to disturb people still asleep on this day of rest. James saw her and waved. She waved back and ran to meet him, through the kissing-gate and down to the lake, slowing down as she reached the treacherous jetty.

'Good morning,' James greeted her with an approving smile. 'Good, you're wearing the right sort of clothes.' He too was waring a thick sweater, but he had waterproof trousers on over his jeans, Romily noticed. 'Here's a pair of waterproof trousers for you. Perhaps you might find them easier to put on on the bank.'

She took the bright yellow plastic trousers and pulled them on. The length was all right, but they were much too big round the waist.

'Who do they belong to? They're huge!' she told him as he helped her on board.

'To a friend who comes out with me when we enter speedboat races. Sorry, I haven't got anything smaller.'

Which meant that he didn't often take female passengers on his boat, Romily surmised, otherwise surely he would have supplied a wetsuit to fit them. He handed her a jacket and this, too, was much too large, but it had elasticated wrists.

'Here's a hat and life-jacket to go with it,' James offered, but Romily shook her head; she wanted to feel the wind in her hair again.

'No, thanks.'

'Afraid I must insist on the life-jacket; you never know when you might hit something in the water and we could go over.'

He helped her on with it and then steered the boat to the far end of the loch and into the mouth of a river which wound its way under a couple of bridges until it emerged into the mile-wide expanse of Loch Ness. Here James opened up the engine and they made good speed over the deep, inhospitable water. At first Romily kept an eye out for the legendary monster, but soon forgot it as she took in the awesome landscape of heather-covered mountains, forever opening to beautiful new vistas of hills and water. They passed Urquhart Castle on their left, the battlemented ruins standing as a monument to the time when the Highlands were ravaged by lost battles and spiteful revenge. And then they reached the far end of the loch where it joined the Caledonian Canal, cut to provide a passage for ships from one coast of Scotland to the other. They went more slowly here so that their wash didn't break down the banks, and at the end there was a whole flight of locks, like giant steps leading from the higher level of the canal down to the sea. And at last they were through and James was opening the throttle as they sped out of the shelter of the Inverness Forth and into the open sea.

The boat hit the first wave and bounced through it, making Romily sway sideways. James put out a restraining arm to hold her, but saw that she had a firm grip on the grab rail and put both hands on the steering wheel again, using his powerful strength to hold the boat on course. They passed other craft, some of them quite big ships making their way to or from the port, and a couple of times they left the surface completely as they hit a bow wave and came crashing down to the sea again. When they did so,

Romily gave a gasping shout of mingled excitement and anticipation, her thrilled face alight with animation. Spray came into the boat, hitting her face, but she hardly noticed it, it was all part of the fun. Deliberately James turned the boat towards the bow wave of a big cargo ship. 'Yes?' he yelled at her, a devilish challenge in his eyes.

'Yes!' she screamed at him. 'Let's go!'

They must have hit the first bow wave sideways on at over a hundred miles an hour. The boat bucketed wildly and for a moment Romily thought that James had lost control, but then they plummeted down the other side and were heading for the second bow-wave. When they were through, she grabbed his arm in intoxicated exhilaration. 'That was fantastic! Let's do it again!' she yelled in his ear.

He laughed and said something, but she didn't hear, so he put a hand at the back of her neck, pulled her to him and kissed her cold, wet face. It wasn't a sexual kiss, but one that expressed his shared love of speed and the feeling that they were more powerful than the elements. He lifted his head after only a moment and they grinned at each other like Cheshire cats, then James let her go and took the boat further out to sea for about ten minutes, before turning to sail parallel to the coast.

But presently dark clouds blew up and it began to rain heavily, so they turned for home. Romily was so wet already that she waved away James's offer of a sou'wester, pushing her wet hair out of her eyes with equally wet hands. But by the time she reached Loch Ness she had begun to shiver, the cold and wet beginning to get to her.

Reaching down to a small locker, James took out

a silver hip flask. 'Here, drink some of this.'

Romily didn't even bother to ask what it was. She unscrewed the top as fast as her numbed fingers would let her and took a deep draught, feeling the fire of brandy as it hit her throat. The warmth licked into her chest and stomach, but she took another swig for good measure before passing it back to James.

'Soon be there now,' he encouraged as they entered the mouth of the river leading to their own loch.

He went as fast as he could in the narrow river and was soon shooting across the lake, but he didn't stop at the jetty below Abbot's Craig as Romily expected him to, instead going on towards the castle. She pulled at his sleeve to remind him, but James shook his head and pointed at a new-looking boathouse and jetty round the bend. He came alongside the jetty and tied up, then cut the boat's engine, the silence suddenly deafening after so much noise for so long. They climbed out on to the jetty, but Romily staggered and would have fallen if James hadn't caught her. She still felt as if she was on the water and for a minute found it impossible to keep her balance on something that kept still.

With his arm round her, James said, 'Come on, let's get you inside and into some dry clothes.' Pushing open the door to the boathouse, he led her inside and she saw that it was full of all the usual boating paraphernalia, but he steered her up a flight of wooden steps to another door which opened into a kind of sitting-room with a big picture window at the end overlooking the lake. An electric fire had been left burning and the pine-panelled room was warm and cosy.

'Here, let me help you off with your waterproofs.'

She had begun to shiver again, so made no demur as James unzipped the jacket and took it off, then bent to pull down the trousers, her hands on his shoulders to steady herself.

'Your hair's soaked. Come and sit by the fire while I get you a towel.'

She obeyed him, her teeth chattering with cold, while he crossed to a cupboard and took out a big, fluffy towel. He gave it to her, then took off his wetsuit, gathered it up with hers and took them down to the floor below to hang to dry.

'Is your sweater wet?' he asked as he came back to kneel down beside her.

'Yes, but only round the neck,' she answered, her voice muffled as she rubbed at her hair.

'Better take it off, then.'

And before she could stop him, James had taken hold of her sweater and was pulling it over her head. 'Hey!' she exclaimed indignantly.

He laughed as he pulled it off. 'You don't want to catch a cold, do you? How about your shirt, is that wet too?'

'No,' she said hastily, putting up a hand to grab the neck together.

He gave her a mocking look. 'Suit yourself, but I'm going to put your sweater to dry and I'm sure you would be far more comfortable if your shirt was dry too.'

Romily gave him a doubtful look. 'What would I wear in the meantime?'

'I'll find you a sweater, I keep several here to change into.' He got up and went to another cupboard. 'This one should do, but it will be rather large, I'm afraid. How about your jeans?'

'They're fine,' Romily said with determination. 'Turn your back.' He raised his eyebrows at her but did as she asked while she took off her shirt and put on his soft sweater. 'Mm, nice,' she commented. 'It looks hand-knitted.'

'It is. Can I turn round now?' She handed her shirt to him and he said tauntingly, 'A lady I know rather well made it for me with her own hands.'

'Lucky you,' Romily said offhandedly, picking up the towel to dry her hair again.

After putting her clothes into an electric drying cabinet James came to kneel beside her on the rug in front of the fire again. 'Your arms must be aching; let me do that for you.'

He reached to take the towel from her, but Romily moved further away. He was becoming a little too free with his offers of help. 'I can manage, thanks,' she said shortly.

'An independent young lady, aren't you?' he said in some amusement, picking up another towel to dry his own hair. 'Most girls like being cosseted a little.'

'I'm not—most girls.'

'So I've noticed.' Throwing the towel on to a long deep settee, he spread out beside her, leaning on one elbow. 'Most girls wouldn't have gone out to sea with me in the boat, or if they had, they would soon have wanted to turn back. But you enjoyed every minute of it.'

'Yes,' Romily agreed, a light of remembered excitement coming into her eyes. 'It was marvellous. I loved it.'

'Then we must do it again some time.'

'Perhaps,' Romily said noncommittally.

'Perhaps,' he mocked, and put up a hand to

gently push aside a lock of hair that lay across her
face. 'Your hair is dry enough now, surely?'

'I suppose so. Do you have a comb?'

'I do, but I like it the way it is, in a tangle of curls
around your head. No, don't try to straighten it.' He
caught hold of her raised hand. 'I'll find a comb for
you before you go home. Now, how about a drink?
I've got a couple of decent bottles of wine in the
fridge.'

Romily looked round the large room, taking note
of the big soft settee, almost as big as a bed, the
curtain that could be closed to shut out the rain, the
drinks trolley and a music centre with a shelf of
records over in the corner. A playboy's pad if ever
she'd seen one. And there was no way she was going
to become just another statistic on that couch!
'Thanks, but I'd rather have coffee,' she said firmly.

James gave her a wry look. 'You know, I've a
feeling you don't trust me,' he remarked as he got to
his feet.

'You could be right at that.'

He plugged in a coffee machine and put in
enough water for two cups. 'Just what did Carol tell
you about me?' he asked.

'I'm sure you don't really want to know.'

'On the contrary, I'd like to know exactly what
she said.' James came to sit on the settee while he
waited for the coffee to heat. 'There's really not
much point in not telling me, is there? I promise you
I won't sue for slander, if that's what you're
worrying about.'

'Hardly. You can only sue for slander when it's a
lie,' she pointed out tartly.

James's mouth twisted into a thin smile. 'So I'm
already prejudged, am I?'

Romily hesitated, not wanting to get involved, not wanting to hear him try to deny it, feeling somehow that she was getting mixed up in something sordid. But she supposed he had a right to know. 'She merely said that you had a shady reputation. That you'd had lots of women in the past and that you were bad news as far as the female sex were concerned.'

'And was that it? She didn't go into details?'

She frowned. 'Isn't it enough?'

'For you, apparently. You obviously believe her.'

Romily looked at him in sudden doubt for a moment, then turned her head away. 'Yes,' she said decisively. 'Yes, I do.'

'Just like that? Without even giving me a hearing?'

Raising her hands in a dismissive gesture, she said forcefully, 'Look, I just don't want to know. I'm—I'm not interested enough to care. OK?' She got agitatedly to her feet. 'I enjoyed going out on your boat with you and I—I enjoy your company. But that's it! I don't want to get involved. So you see, it really doesn't matter about your murky past.'

James sat watching her until she had finished, an assessing look in his eyes. 'I see,' he said slowly. 'So all you want is friendship?'

'Friendship would do fine.' She looked at him in some surprise; she had expected him to be angry, especially about the murky past bit, but he didn't seem to be at all put out. Still not quite trusting him, she said doggedly, 'But that's all. No—no sex.'

A pained expression came into James's eyes. 'I wouldn't let it rear its ugly head,' he vowed solemnly.

Romily's mouth puckered and then she had to

smile. 'Do you always make people laugh when they're trying to be serious?'

'Always. You see, people do tend to take themselves so very seriously.'

'But you don't?'

'Myself, d'you mean? Or other people?' The light went out on the coffee machine and he got up to pour it out, adding a shot of Scotch whisky. 'I seem to remember you said you didn't have a boyfriend.'

'No.' Romily took the mug of coffee from him.

'But there has been one in the past?' She raised quick, questioning eyes to his face and he gave a small shrug. 'It's pretty obvious. When a girl declares that she's off men it usually means that she's been hurt. Am I right?'

'Mind your own damn business!'

'I see I am,' he remarked easily. 'Who was he?'

Romily glowered at him and went to put down her mug.

'All right,' James held up his hand, 'I won't ask any more questions. Except one.'

She glared at him. 'You don't expect me to answer it, do you?'

'Not unless you want to.' He grinned at her. 'I was merely going to ask how you liked your steak cooked.'

'Steak?' She looked at him in some bewilderment, not sure if he was being serious.

'Mm. I'm hungry, aren't you?' He pointed to an old brass ship's clock on the wall. 'Look, it's almost two o'clock, time we had some lunch. Though it's only steak and a salad, I'm afraid. I don't claim to be any good at cooking.' Getting to his feet, James went to the far end of the room where one of the pine-fronted cupboards turned out to be a fridge and another a pull-down grill.

Romily watched as he began to prepare the meal, her anger still simmering. He had no right to ask her questions about her personal life. She had half a mind to just walk out. But it was raining outside, and she was hungry, and she was wearing his clothes. A thought occurred to her and she looked at him again, wondering if he had asked those probing questions because she had repeated what Carol had said about *his* private life.

Glancing round, he caught her eyes on him. 'You look very pensive. How about coming to keep an eye on the steaks while I toss the salad?'

Slowly Romily got to her feet and joined him. She saw at a glance that he didn't really need her help, he was managing very efficiently on his own, tossing the salad with an experienced hand. Belatedly she remembered that he was her host. 'I'm sorry if I offended you,' she said stiffly. 'But you asked me what Carol had said about you, and I merely repeated it.'

'I'm not offended. It doesn't matter to me what Car— what other people say. I was just disappointed that you were so willing to damn me on hearsay evidence.'

'But if you don't care what other people think of you, why should it bother you what I think?' she asked curiously.

James gave her a quick look, then shrugged. 'Why, indeed? But, strangely, it does. There, the salad's ready. How about the steaks?'

'How do you like yours?'

'Medium rare.'

'They're done, then.'

'They carried the plates over to a small table set

near the window and James poured chilled wine
into crystal glasses, then put a cassette in the music
centre. The sweet notes of a saxophone playing a
classical jazz tune rippled from the speakers, soon
joined by other instruments until a whole band was
playing. Romily had cut into her steak and was
about to eat, but this tape had been one of Richard's
favourites, too; he had often played it when he had
parked the car in some quiet spot and reached out to
take her in his arms and love her. Putting down her
fork, she said curtly, 'Do you mind playing
something else?'

'Of course not. Don't you like jazz?'

'Not much.'

Reaching out, he ejected the tape and put in
another, of ordinary ballads by a well-known singer
this time. 'All right?'

She nodded and picked up her fork again, but
somehow her appetite had gone. She sat looking
down at her plate in sad-eyed remembrance.

'Is it that bad?'

Looking up, she saw that James was gesturing
towards her steak. 'Oh no, of course not, It's very
good. Who taught you to cook, the same lady who
knitted this sweater for you?'

He gave a rather devilish grin, as if at some
private joke. 'As a matter of fact, she did.'

Was he then so proud of his conquests that he
boasted about them? But Romily dismissed the
idea; no playboy ever boasted about being taught to
cook. That thought made her realise that, apart
from that, James had never talked about other
women at all, except in very general terms as
anyone would.

'Do you have any family?' she asked curiously.

He shook his head. 'A couple of aunts and some cousins, but no one nearer than that.'

'So you live in the castle alone?' He nodded and she said, 'Don't you find it awfully big for you?'

'Much too big,' he agreed, picking up his glass. 'But I hope to fill it a little more some day.'

So he wanted a family, did he? But he was hardly going the right way about it, Romily thought wryly. 'Aren't you leaving it a little—er—late?'

He laughed. 'You don't pull your punches, do you? Possibly you're right. But I've never felt like settling for a rock bun when there might be a cream cake somewhere along the way.'

Romily burst into laughter. 'What a terrible simile! And anyway, surely you'd rather have a Scottish bannock?'

'Not necessarily.' His amused eyes settled on her face, changing to an arrested expression. 'You look very lovely when you laugh. You ought to do it all the time.'

'That's ridiculous! My hair's a mess and I haven't got a scrap of make-up on,' Romily protested.

'You look great,' he corrected her firmly. 'Clean and natural and animated, full of life. As you ought to be. Not as you sometimes are when you have that sad face.'

'Nonsense. I'm never sad,' Romily lied. 'Probably I was thinking about what to have for dinner.'

James let it go and they talked of other things for a few moments until Romily mentioned having been to see Maggie again.

'So we'll be able to have real Scots porridge on the menu now,' she told him.

'You're really keen on this traditional food idea, aren't you?'

'Yes, I am. There are hundreds of hotels in Scotland so we must be something special to make people choose to stay with us.'

'And do you think you'll enjoy working here?'

'Oh, yes. It will be nice to have the whole meals to prepare, not just one course.'

'You get on all right with Carol and your brother, then?'

There was something in his tone that made Romily turn her head to look at him. They had finished eating and were sitting on the couch at a sedate distance apart, finishing the wine. 'Yes, of course,' she answered coolly. 'Why shouldn't I?'

'No reason. I was just curious as you couldn't know them that well. Unless you lived abroad with them?'

'No, I didn't. I was at college in London and then working in various hotels most of the time they were away.'

'And did you live in the hotels?'

'Oh, yes.'

'So you haven't had a proper home for years?'

With a light laugh, Romily said, 'You get used to that with hotel work. Most of the time you have a room to yourself, so you do get some privacy.'

'It sounds a very lonely life,' James remarked as he got up to put on a new cassette and refill her glass from a fresh bottle of wine.

'No more than yours,' Romily retaliated, feeling on the defensive. Getting off the couch, she pulled a cushion on to the floor and sat on it, leaning her back against the settee. She felt beautifully warm now, and pleasantly full. The wine and the music, too, were making her feel drowsy and contented.

James stretched out full length on the settee

behind her, his glass in his hand, but presently he began to stroke her hair, gently combing out the tangles with his fingers. She let him do it for a moment and then straightened up, but he caught her shoulder and pulled her back. 'Relax,' he said softly, and went on playing with her hair. It was nice, Romily liked it, and she felt so peaceful and warm. After a while, though, his fingers moved to stroke the skin of her neck, his touch feather-light and tantalising. 'Why don't you come up here and join me?' he suggested. 'It's much more comfortable than the floor.'

Romily didn't even consider it for a moment, just got to her feet in a lithe, graceful movement. 'Sorry to spoil your fun, but I have to be getting back.'

She turned to move away, but James caught her hand. 'Romily! Just come and be comfortable, that's all. You *can* trust me, you know.'

'Can I?' she retorted unbelievingly.

'Why not give it a try? You can always leave when you want to.'

She looked at him doubtfully, recognising his masculine attraction and not sure if she had sufficient control of herself at the moment to resist it if he made a pass. He gave her a gentle pull and against her will she let him draw her down on to the settee beside him. He was right, it was extremely confortable. She lay down and James put his arm beneath her neck, but that was all.

'Now,' he instructed, 'just close your eyes and relax. Listen to the music.'

Obediently she closed her eyes, but found it impossible to relax when he was so close. Her senses were alert as she waited, sure that he would start to touch her and ready to jump to her feet if he did, but

the minutes passed without him doing so and
gradually her drowsy senses relaxed until she fell
asleep.

When she awoke almost an hour later, she found
that James, too, was asleep, but in his sleep he had
put his arms round her and was now holding her
very close. She gave a little jerk of startled surprise
and he moved a little, his arms tightening; he
murmured something that sounded like 'Darling',
but didn't waken.

Romily looked at his face, so close to her own,
indignantly, wondering if he had touched her while
she was asleep. But she hadn't been *that* tired; she
would have known if he'd handled her. It was
obvious that he was used to sleeping with a woman
from the natural way he held her, and that murmur
in his sleep had been a dead giveaway. For a
moment she felt angry, but then grinned as she
thought that this was probably the first time in his
life that he had slept with a woman without making
love to her. But it was time he woke up so that she
could go home, so she blew in his face. His eyelids
flickered and he stirred but didn't wake, but before
she could do it again, he murmured something else,
leaned forward and kissed her!

Romily was taken by surprise and it took her a
moment to recover sufficiently to try to push him
away. 'Hey,' she mumbled indignantly againt his
mouth, 'wake up!'

It took longer than she'd thought possible for him
to wake, his mouth and arms holding her tenacious-
ly, and she had to thump him in the ribs a couple of
times before he finally opened his eyes. 'Oh, hallo.'
He blinked at her. 'Sorry, did I roll on you?' He
moved away. 'Must have fallen asleep too. I was

having the most wonderful dream.'

'Were you, indeed?' Romily exclaimed indignantly, sitting up.

'Mm. Trouble is, it's gone completely now. I wonder what it was?' But then he shrugged. 'You went out like a light.'

She looked at him suspiciously, wondering if he really hadn't known that he was kissing her. 'I have to get home,' she told him coldly.

'Yes, of course.' He got to his feet at once. 'I'll get your things for you. And when you've changed I'll run you home in the car.'

He began to clear the table while she put on her dry clothes, beautifully warm from the drying cabinet, so she didn't have to tell him to turn his back this time. 'You promised me a comb,' she reminded him.

'Of course.' He found one for her and she combed her hair in a mirror.' Now you're respectable again,' he commented. 'Ready?'

They ran from the boathouse door to the car through the rain that was still falling quite heavily, and James drove past the castle to the road and down the short way to Abbot's Craig, taking her all the way down the drive to the entrance to the courtyard. He would have driven in, but Romily stopped him. 'This will do, thanks.'

'Right.' It was almost dark now, she could hardly see his face as he turned to her and said, 'Afraid to be seen with me?'

Slowly she said, 'It avoids—complications.'

He gave a rather grim laugh, but said, 'Fair enough. When will you come out with me again?

'On the boat, do you mean?'

'No, out to dinner.' Adding when she hesitated, 'I

should point out that I did keep my word today. We were just friends enjoying ourselves together, right?'

Romily nodded. And it had been fun, so why not do it again?' 'Dinner on the same terms?'

'Whatever you want,' he agreed.

'All right, then. How about Wednesday?'

'Fine. I'll come down to the house and pick you up at seven-thirty, shall I?'

She immediately shook her head. 'No, I'll meet you at the top of the drive, same as last time.' Opening the door of the car, she said. 'Thanks for the boat ride and everything. Goodnight.'

'Goodnight, Romily. Oh . . .' He leaned across the car as she was getting out. 'And thanks for making my dream come true. It was quite something.'

Her eyes widened as she realised that he'd been awake all the time he'd been kissing her, but before she could say anything he had pulled the door to, and driven off with a wave and a wicked grin!

Carol and Gerald were upstairs working on their flat again. Romily called up to them that she was home and then went up to her room, but she hadn't been there very long before Carol gave a tap on the door and came in. 'Hallo. Had a good day?'

'Mm, not bad. How was your party last night? I didn't even hear you come home.'

'No, it was nearly four by the time we got to bed. I'm afraid we had a bit too much to drink, but we really enjoyed ourselves. It was the first time I've really felt in the swing of things since we came back to Scotland. Lots of our old friends were there.' Carol went on talking about the party, the frown of worry about the hotel quite gone as she described it.

'And they were all terribly interested in the hotel
project and promised to help all they could by
advertising and that kind of thing. Some of them
even said that they might come to dinner here
instead of going to a restaurant in Inverness. I
explained that we hadn't really thought about
catering for other than the hotel guests, but it's quite
an idea. What do you think?'

Romily took time before she answered, realising
that it would probably mean a whole lot more work
for her. Also, she could envisage them deciding to
keep the place open as a restaurant during the
winter instead of closing down completely, which
was entirely different from what she'd anticipated.
'How many would you expect to cater for?' she
asked warily.

'Well, the dining-room holds twenty-two, and we
could put another table for four or six in that little
hallway that leads out to the terrace if we block the
door off. That would be twenty-eight at the very
most, and there would only be one sitting, of
course.'

I should hope so, Romily thought wryly. Decisively she said, 'I think you'd have to give me at least
a month after we've opened to settle in before you
start the idea. And if there are any more than twelve
people in to dinner, then I should have to have help
in the kitchen in preparing the meals as well as
actually cooking them.'

'I said I'd help in the kitchen,' Carol pointed out.

'You can help in the preparation, certainly. But
you can't act as waitress and help to cook as well;
we'd get in a hopeless muddle. And anyway, in a
hotel like this you'd probably find that everyone
wanted to eat at the same time. If that's all right,

then I'll be happy to give it a try.'

'That's marvellous!' Carol's face lit up. 'I'll tell
Gerald.' She began to walk towards the door, then
stopped. 'Oh, and we thought that we might have a
party—a sort of hotel-warming a little later in the
year. It will give you a chance to meet our friends.'

'Fine,' Romily agreed. 'Whenever you like.'

'We'll have to work out a day when we think we
won't be too busy. Where did you go today, by the
way?'

'Into Inverness,' said Romily in a half-truth.

Carol wrinkled her nose. 'The place is dead on a
Sunday. What on earth did you find to do?'

'I—er—looked at the boats in the harbour.'

'Good heavens! All day?'

'No, I ate out and listened to some music.'

'You're lucky, there was nothing open at all on a
Sunday when I was your age,' Carol told her, her
mind obviously too full of her own schemes to take
much notice. 'See you later.'

'OK.' Romily sat back in her chair and propped
her feet up on the bed, wondering why she had lied
to Carol. No, not lied, just let her believe what was
far from being the whole truth. But right now
Romily wanted to keep her outing with James to
herself; not only because she knew Carol would
disapprove, but also because she just wasn't in a
secure enough state, mentally and emotionally to
discuss her private affairs with anyone. But it had
been fun today. A small smile played around her
mouth as she remembered. And James had been
good company, *and* kept his word, except for that
stolen kiss. Her smile widened. It had felt right
being with him, and she was looking forward to
seeing him again on Wednesday. That thought

quite startled her; she hadn't expected to feel contented in a man's company ever again.

The clocks had been adjusted for summer time and the evenings were lighter, but at seven-thirty on Wednesday evening it was still dark enough to need a torch to light her way up the drive. Tonight she had taken trouble with her appearance, washing her hair and putting on one of her newest outfits. She felt good and was alive with anticipation, wondering where James was going to take her.

He was already at the road, leaning against his car and waiting patiently for her. 'Hi,' he greeted her. 'Am I allowed to kiss you yet?'

'Certainly not!' she rebuked him, but there was no severity in her tone.

He grinned at her as he opened the passenger door. 'A man has to try! You might have had a change of heart since I saw you last.'

She raised her eyebrows at him. 'Now why on earth should I do that?'

He looked crestfallen as he got in the car beside her, but it was only pretence. 'You're a hard woman, Romily Bennion.'

'Of course I am,' she agreed, trying to look hard and failing completely. 'What else did you expect?'

James looked at her, his eyes alight with laughter, but slowly the laughter died, his eyes lit by an entirely different emotion. 'I wish you'd learn to trust me,' he said softly.

Romily met his look for a moment, then deliberately turned away, her cheeks flushed. 'Where are we going?'

His lips twisting in self-mockery, he said, 'To the theatre.'

They did go to the theatre, but not to see a show; instead going to a restaurant called The Bishop's Table in the Eden Court Theatre, where they helped themselves from a sumptuous buffet. They sat at a table beside a big window looking over the River Ness, the twinkling lights of this capital of the Highlands spread out before them. There was unobtrusive music that formed a background to the murmur of voices and the chink of cutlery in the large room, but they were able to talk comfortably, finding interests they had in common other than the love of speed. James, too, liked to walk, but he had done some really tough ones, like walking from one side of England to the other on Hadrian's Wall, the wall the Romans had built to keep the barbarian Scottish tribes out of England. 'I'd like to do that new coastal walk round the South of England one day,' he told her.

'Mm, and I've always wanted to walk the Pilgrims' Way, the route that Chaucer took to Canterbury,' Romily enthused.

'So why don't you?'

She shrugged. 'Maybe I will one day. It's rather a long way from Scotland.'

'But not far from London. Why haven't you done it already?'

Picking up a fork, she traced a pattern on the tablecloth, her face shadowed. 'I've never had the opportunity,' she evaded.

James watched her speculatively, but she didn't raise her head, and after a moment he went on to talk of something else.

Their meal over, they went back to the car and

James took the now familiar road out of Inverness. Romily felt a little stab of disappointment. It was still early and she didn't want the evening to end yet. It was too early to go home and go to bed. And the hotel was due to open next Tuesday, so this would probably be her last opportunity to have an evening out for ages. She almost said as much to James, but held her tongue; maybe he was tired of her company. She bit her lip; the raw loss of confidence that she had experienced after Richard returning to make her hold her hands tightly together in her lap.

But her feelings did a complete about-turn as James drove calmly past the driveway to Abbot's Craig. He's taking me to his boathouse again, she thought wildly, and prepared to be angry and stand-offish, but he went past the track leading down to the lake, too, and she looked at him with questioning eyes.

He drew up outside the castle and returned her look mockingly, apparently fully aware of what she'd been thinking. 'Welcome to my castle, fair maiden,' he said teasingly.

Slowly she relaxed and smiled. 'Will I find any dragons there, sir knight?'

'I've driven them all away.' Lifting his hand, he gently stroked her cheek. 'There's nothing there that will harm you.'

'And you won't lock me in the highest room your topmost turret?' she asked, perhaps only half jokingly.

'Ah, would that I could.' He looked rueful. 'But I've a feeling you'd scream the walls down!' Getting out of the car, he opened her door for her, then took her hand to walk her across the stone bridge that replaced the old drawbridge that had lain across the now green-lawned moat.

CHAPTER FIVE

IT was a small castle as castles go. They went through an archway into a well-lit courtyard that had ferns growing against the walls among old millstones, and there was an old lead water butt full of plants. On the right there was a wide wooden door with a coat of arms carved in stone above it, which led to a passageway and on into what must once have been the great hall but was now a pleasantly furnished drawing-room. The room was very high, with a ceiling of great pine beams and at one end a minstrel gallery hung with a heraldic tapestry. At the other end was a huge, unlit fireplace, although the room felt pleasantly warm, which was strange because it should have felt cold being so high and with so much stonework, but there were thick peach-coloured velvet curtains at the windows and a fitted carpet on the floor which took any echoing emptiness away. The room was brightly lit by many lamps and the furniture was light, complementing the many colourful portraits on the walls in their rich gold frames.

Romily looked round the room and immediately became awestruck; she had worked in many luxurious hotels, but this was James's home, for heaven's sake! 'It's—er—very nice,' she managed inadequately.

With an amused grin, James took her hand and led her up a twisting stone staircase built into a narrow turret to show her the rest of the house. He took her into rooms hung with rich tapestries, into passages adorned with displays of ancient weapons, down to a dark dungeon with chains embedded in the walls, into an old kitchen still hung with glowing copper pans and jugs, and into a bedroom with a four-poster bed with a headboard of sumptuously carved and painted acanthus leaves.

Romily had been silent most of the time, but now she exclaimed in spellbound wonder, 'My God, do you really sleep in that?'

James laughed. 'Only on very special occasions. If I slept in it regularly it would probably fall to bits. I have a very much more modern bed in my own room. Would you like to see it?'

Shaking her head, Romily said lightly, 'Thanks, but I'm already overwhelmed. How do you find time to use all these rooms?'

'You grow into them, I suppose,' he shrugged. 'Let's go up to my sitting-room and have a drink.'

She could tell at once that this was the room he used most. There were shelves full of books and magazines and a desk with trays of letters and other paperwork. And here there was a fire blazing welcomingly in the Victorian-looking fireplace.

'This is part of the wing that one of my ancestors built on in the nineteenth century,' James explained. 'I like it because it looks out over the gardens and the burn.'

'The what?' Romily asked with a puzzled frown.

Coming up to her, he put an arm around her waist and led her towards a dusty-pink upholstered love-seat, set her down in it and put his hands on her shoulders. 'A burn, you lovely Sassenach, is a brook or small river. If you listen, you'll be able to hear it running below the castle walls. Now, what would you like to drink?'

'Do you have sherry and tonic water?'

He raised his eyes to heaven. 'My God, what a mixture! But a sherry and tonic you shall have.'

While he went to fix it, Romily closed her eyes and listened hard. And yes, that faint noise that was always in the background could be the rustling of water over stones.

'Romily.' She opened her eyes to see James standing over her with a drink in his hand. He gave it to her and went to sit in the other half of the love-seat, so that they were facing opposite ways but their heads were close together. 'What do you think of the place?' he asked as he sipped his own drink.

'As I said, overwhelming. I didn't know that places like this existed in private ownership. I thought they'd all been taken over by the National Trust.'

'You'd be surprised; there's still quite a few of us who manage to hang on to our homes, mainly because of good husbandry by our ancestors, who took care to make the estate productive and viable, and married rich heiresses when they got desperate,' he added with a grin.

Romily wanted to ask him if he was desperate, but instead pointed to a painting on the wall of a man in full tartan dress. 'Who was that?'

'An ancestor who was a staunch Jacobite. He had that portrait painted in 1762, wearing the tartan as an act of defiance when all Scotsmen were banned from wearing it after the battle of Culloden.' He nodded to a ring of claymores on the wall. 'That's where all those came from. It's only a few miles from here.'

'From the actual battlefield?' He nodded without

speaking, and after a moment Romily said stiffly,
'Is that why you dislike the English so much?'

He raised a surprised eyebrow. 'What makes you
think I dislike the English?'

'You said that you didn't want them invading the
Highlands.'

With a shake of his head, James said, 'No, I said I
didn't want hordes of tourists. We get people
coming here from all over the world, and from
lowland Scotland, too. I'm not anti-English. Some
of them I even find quite fascinating,' he murmured, his eyes darkening as he looked at her. 'I'm
sorry, Romily,' he said thickly, 'but I'm just going to
have to kiss you.' And leaning forward he sought
her mouth with his.

She could easily have moved her head away, and
for a moment intended to do so, but the urgent,
seeking need of his lips was irresistible and she let
him take her mouth. But she held herself stiffly,
poised to move away, her head rigid and making no
response. James kissed her with restrained hunger,
his lips exploring hers yearningly, touching, caress-
ing, trying to awaken a reaction yet frightened of
scaring her off.

It was so long since she had been kissed like that.
She sat numbly, letting him do what he wanted, all
her senses and emotions concentrated in the feel of
his lips on hers. Gently he tried to open her mouth,
but she kept hers firmly closed and he didn't try to
push her, instead covering her lips with small kisses
and then touching them lightly with his tongue. It
was only their mouths that touched, he didn't try to
put his arms round her or anything, and somehow
this total concentration on what he was doing to her
lips slowly got to her. Romily gave a long sigh and

slowly opened her mouth under his, tilting her head back as she began to respond at last.

She felt the quiver of mingled pleasure and triumph that ran through him, and then James was kissing her with ever-deepening passion, avidly exploring the inner moistness of her mouth, his hunger for her let loose now as he kissed her with ardent yearning.

He was reluctant ever to let her go, but eventually they broke apart, their breathing ragged, Romily slowly opening her eyes to stare at him in bemusement.

James's eyes were still dark with need and he was breathing rather unsteadily as he said huskily, 'Thank you.' Adding when she didn't speak, 'For trusting yourself to me at last.'

Immediately Romily got agitatedly to her feet and walked away from him. 'Just because I let you kiss me it doesn't mean—doesn't mean that I . . .'

James, too, got to his feet, put down his glass and came over to her. 'Doesn't mean what?' he asked, taking her glass from her and setting it down.

'That I'm going to go to bed with you,' Romily told him baldly, backing away from him.

He gave a short laugh. 'I wasn't aware that I'd asked you to.'

'But you were going to,' she retorted. 'A man doesn't kiss a girl like that unless he wants her.'

James's eyes shadowed. 'And have many men kissed you like that, Romily?'

Her face flushed with anger. 'And just how many women have you kissed like that this year? This month? This week?' She turned to stride from the room, but James caught her wrist and pulled her back, his face set.

'Not nearly as many as you've damn well been led to believe,' he said forcefully. 'OK, I used to play the field when I was younger, and there have been a few women in the last ten years, but I'm no—no libertine. I'm a man of my time, Romily, and this age isn't exactly noted for its prudery.' His blue eyes met her challengingly. 'As I think you know for yourself.'

She broke free from him and turned away, only too painfully aware that he was right.

'Look,' James said more softly, coming up behind her and putting his hands on her shoulders, 'what's the point in arguing over something as useless as the past. Sure, maybe we've both been around, so why don't we just . . .'

'No!' She turned fiercely to face him. 'I'm not promiscuous! I don't—don't . . .'

'Go with men,' he finished for her. Adding, to her surprise, 'Good, I'm glad to hear it. Now I know I really earned that kiss.'

She looked at him uncertainly, not knowing how to take it. 'I told you before, I don't want to get involved.'

He nodded. 'So I remember.' Taking her hand, he gently drew her towards him and put his arm round her. 'But then we hadn't done this properly before, had we?' And he kissed her again, slowly drawing her closer against him until their bodies were touching.

Romily trembled, feeling the closeness of his hard, muscled body, remembering another man, another body, holding her close. But gradually as he kissed her memory faded, to be replaced by the heady, sensuous sensations of the present. James wasn't Richard. James was a different kind of lover

entirely, willing to give as well as take, to arouse her
senses with lingering kisses that made the warmth
of need grow in the pit of her stomach and her
breath catch in her throat. Putting his hand low on
her waist, he moulded her body to his, curving her
against him, holding her as a woman should be held
when she's being kissed, so that she was aware that
he wanted her. Almost against her will, her body
moved against him, her lips telling their own
message of desire.

James's lips left hers to explore her neck and
nuzzle at her earlobe. Her head tilted back as he
kissed the long column of her throat, her nails
digging into his shoulders as she clung to him, her
eyes closed, her breath a moaning purr of pleasure
and need.

Lifting his head, James said, 'Romily.' And then
more urgently, 'Romily, look at me!'

Slowly she did so, to find his blue eyes smiling
down at her.

'My darling, I think that you're involved with me
whether you like it or not.' His smile deepened, his
eyes crinkling at the corners. 'But something tells
me that you do like it—just a little?'

The way they were standing, with their bodies so
close together, there could be little doubt of that,
and it made Romily smile too. But then the smile
faded and she lowered her head.

'Oh, no, you don't!' James put his hand under her
chin so that she had to look at him again. 'I don't
want you ever to turn away from me again. Or to
look sad. I hate it when you withdraw from me with
that sad look on your face, and I know that you're
remembering the past.' His hands tightened on her.
'It makes me want to kill the bastard that hurt you!'

He spoke so fiercely that it startled her. Her eyes searched his face, still afraid to believe that he might care for her or want her for anything other than sex.

'Who was he, darling? What did he do to you?' James demanded. 'Please tell me.'

Romily didn't attempt to deny that he was right, but she said slowly, 'Why do you want to know?'

'So that I can understand. So that I can help you to forget. To heal the wounds.'

But that was going too far. She shook her head decisively. 'There's nothing to tell.'

'Oh, but I'm certain there is.' Looking down at her earnestly, James said, 'You've trusted me so far, Romily. Won't you trust me completely?'

But Romily was the kind of girl who kept her hurts to herself, even though they might fester more that way and take a very long time for the scars to fade. Pushing herself free from his hold, she said, 'You keep talking about trust all the time. So I let you kiss me; I'm sure it meant as little to you as it did to me. Kisses don't mean anything any more.'

'You may be convincing yourself of that, but you're certainly not convincing me. They meant something to me. And I'm pretty certain they did to you too. But maybe you'd like another demonstration.' And he stepped purposefully towards her.

'No!' She put up her hands to hold him off. 'All right, I—I admit they meant something. But I'm not ready to—to ...'

Immediately James put his arms round her and held her against him, his hand stroking her hair. 'It's all right—don't worry. We've got plenty of time.' He smiled at her. 'All the time in the world.'

His words reassured her and she relaxed against

him, enjoyed being held, feeling the strength of his arms around her and the strange sense of comfort and security it gave her. She felt him kiss her hair, but soon he sought her mouth again, this time awakening an immediate response if not an answering passion. They kissed for some time, but when James tried to lead her towards a settee, she resisted him, shaking her head and saying. 'I think I'd better go,' in an unsteady voice.

But when he drove her back to Abbot's Craig, James insisted on kissing her goodnight. 'When can I see you again?' he murmured against her throat. 'Tomorrow?'

'I can't make tomorrow night. I promised to help Gerald type out the fire regulations to put in the bedrooms.'

'During the day, then. Come up to Maggie's. I'll meet you there.'

'I'll try,' she agreed, feeling his breath, hot on her skin. 'But I can't promise.'

'If you're not there tomorrow, I'll phone you.'

'No, don't do that. I'll—I'll phone you.'

He let her go at last and she ran up to her room, her thoughts and emotions in a confused whirl, but when she went to bed that night, Romily's last thoughts were to wonder who had knitted him his sweater, and who was the woman he shared his sumptuous bed with on those special occasions.

James was waiting for her when she went to Maggie's the next day and walked back with her through the woods, kissing her as soon as they were out of sight, and this time making full use of the kissing-gate. His lips were avid with hunger, but if Romily felt any passion she didn't give way to it, responding but not enough to arouse him into uncontrollable emotion. She liked his kisses and was content to return them, feeling her way slowly into this new relationship that James was so eager for.

On Saturday evening she managed to get away to go out with him again, although she felt rather guilty about it because Gerald and Carol were working flat out on all the last minute details before the first guests arrived on Tuesday. But she justified her actions to herself because she knew that once the hotel opened she would get very few more evenings off until it closed in October. She also felt that she had to point this out to Carol, who merely nodded rather wearily and said, 'Who is the boyfriend you've got in Inverness? You'll have to invite him out here so we can meet him.'

'Yes. Maybe—maybe I'll do that,' Romily answered, and escaped to run through the windswept evening to where James was waiting for her at the top of the drive. He strode to meet her, enfolding her in his arms as he kissed her long and lingeringly. 'Your nose is cold,' she complained, to cover the flushed and breathless state he left her in.

'Which proves that I'm a good healthy specimen. You ought to snap me up at once,' he told her as they got in the car.

'But I'm not in the market for a dog,' she pointed out demurely, enjoying flirting with him.

'Ah, but think how nice it would be to take me for walks every day. And you could even tuck me into bed every night.' he said suggestively.

Her ripple of laughter set the tone for the evening. James took her to a dance in a hotel in Fort William and they laughed and drank and danced, James often flirting with her outrageously. She pretended to scold him, but for the first time in months she felt really carefree again, forgetting all about the past in this strange sort of excitement she was beginning to feel when she was with him. They danced till one and drove contentedly through the starlit night, listening to music on the cassette player during the long drive home.

When they neared the top of the driveway to Abbot's Craig James slowed the car. 'Home—or back to the castle for a while?' he asked her.

Romily hesitated, afraid that he would want to make love to her. Part of her wanted that; her body was fully awake now to the delight that came when he kissed her and was more than ready for the fulfilment of that need, but her mind was still afraid of being hurt again, of being cast aside as soon as he'd grown tired of her.

She hesitated too long; James turned the car down the driveway to take her home. 'Well, at least you didn't give me an outright no,' he said resignedly.

'I'm—I'm sorry.'

'Are you? Really?' He stopped the car as usual just outside the courtyard where no one could see them from the house.

'Yes.'

'Oh, my darling girl!' Catching hold of her, he kissed her with a fierce hunger that betrayed his burning need for her and the iron self-control he was having to exert. 'If you only knew how much I want you!'

Romily was beginning to get the idea and her legs were a little shaky as she let herself into the house. But she felt good, and life was definitely worth living again.

The first guests, a group of American tourists from New York, arrived on the following Tuesday and seemed to like the country-house atmosphere that Carol and Gerald had tried to create. There were teething troubles, of course, but on the whole things went quite smoothly, but it was more difficult for Romily to get away as other guests arrived to take the place of the first.

Luckily they didn't serve lunches, so she did have a few hours off on the days when she didn't have to go shopping, usually with Gerald, into Inverness. On those days she would get through her work as quickly as she could, clearing up after breakfast and preparing what she had to for dinner, before hurrying to change and go out. She didn't go so often to Maggie's now, or if she did she left much earlier, pleading work as an excuse. Often she would just phone James and run through the woods to meet him, sometimes at the boathouse, sometimes at the castle. Once she heard Carol and Gerald talking about her and wondering where she went, and had to put a hand to her mouth to stop herself from laughing when Gerald asserted the opinion that she was meeting Ian MacPherson at Maggie's house.

'But why doesn't she say so?' asked Carol.

'Well, you know how shy Ian is; he probably won't let her for fear of it going all round the neighbourhood.'

It rained a lot that spring and wasn't the kind of weather to go out on the boat, and neither James nor Romily wanted to spend their snatched hours together in Inverness among hundreds of other people, so they usually sat in James's room in the castle drinking coffee and talking, or down in the boathouse on the big settee. In some ways Romily liked the boathouse best because she felt more alone with him there. He had a married couple working for him at the castle and a couple of times one of them had knocked on the door while she was there, which tended to make James curse under his breath and be more circumspect when he kissed her. But at the boathouse there was nothing to stop him from kissing her for as long and as often as he wanted. They lay together on the big settee, listening to the rain beating against the wooden roof as James's knowing hands gradually explored her more and more.

He murmured endearments against her mouth, told her in words and with his eyes that she was lovely. His hands unbuttoned her shirt, performing their own ritual to reveal her breasts to his gaze and the caresses of his hands and lips. Romily's breath gasped in her throat and her hands twisted in his hair as he took her in his mouth, sucking, gently biting, until her body writhed in mingled ecstasy and frustration. He was very experienced, able to raise her senses to fever pitch and hold her there until she gasped out his name in a frenzy of desire. But he didn't try to touch her anywhere else, although his lovemaking must have made James achingly frustrated too. And vaguely Romily knew that he wouldn't go further unless she encouraged him to, that she only had to say yes and he would love her completely.

She could only guess at the discipline he had to exert over himself on their stolen afternoons, but was grateful for it. She was learning to love again and to lose her fear of being hurt, but she wasn't ready yet to commit herself completely. As James had said, they had all the time in the world.

There was only one thing that marred her growing happiness. Several times James had asked her if she had told Carol and Gerald that she was seeing him, and now he was starting to grow insistent.

'Does it matter so much?' she protested. 'Why do you want them to know?'

'Because ours isn't some hole-and-corner affair. I want to be able to call for you at the house instead of letting you walk through the rain to meet me. We're both free, Romily. We have nothing to be afraid or ashamed of.'

There was urgency in his voice and she wanted to please him, but there were undefined reasons that held her back. Possibly the basic reason was the deep fear of being made a fool of again, of having everyone know if James let her down as Richard had done. And perhaps the secrecy enhanced the excitement, added to her rising heartbeat when she knew that she was going to meet him. Or perhaps it was just a wish to keep him to herself. And there was always the fact that Carol didn't approve of him. But she only spoke of the latter, using it as her excuse.

'To hell with what Carol thinks,' James said forcefully. 'It's how we feel that matters. Promise me you'll tell them.'

Slowly Romily said, 'But what's the point? If it's nothing to do with them, why bother to tell them?'

Putting his arm round her, he drew her closer. 'I want them to know. I want to know—what form their disapproval is going to take. So that we can overcome it.'

Romily turned her head to look at him in surprise. 'But surely all they can do is to say they don't like it. They're hardly likely to kick me out or anything because of it. Anything like that would be archaic. And besides, they'd never be able to get another cook to replace me at such short notice,' she added practically.

'So if all they're going to do is say they disapprove, why are you so reluctant to tell them?' James asked insistently.

She wrinkled her nose. 'I don't know. Because it's not their business, I suppose. And because there's— there's nothing really to tell. Only that we're seeing each other.'

'It's more than that and you know it. Don't you?' He bent his head to find her mouth. 'Don't you?' he insisted against her lips.

'Yes,' she breathed, for the first time admitting in words what she had already begun to recognise in her heart.

It was raining yet again. As Romily looked out of the window she wondered why on earth anyone ever bothered to visit the Scottish Highlands at all. And yet they did, from all over the world and in droves, if the number of guests they were getting at the hotel was anything to go by. Resignedly but eagerly, she pulled on wellington boots and mac; James had had to go away on business and this was the first time they had been able to meet in over a week.

'Going out?' asked Gerald in surprise as he came into the passage off the kitchen where she was sitting to pull on her boots. 'It's absolutely pouring outside'

'Yes, I know. I'm—I'm going up to Maggie's. She's promised to teach me how to make another dish.' Which was a lie and made her feel a bit guilty, but she thought that Gerald was busy and not really interested.

But he refuted her by saying, 'What are you going to make? We might be able to put it on the menu next week.'

'Er—Cullen Skink.'

'Good God, what's that? It sounds revolting.'

'I don't really know yet.' She stood up.

Gerald looked her over. 'You're not walking, are you? Why don't you take the car?'

'It's—it's broken down,' she fabricated, unable to tell him that James would be waiting for her in the woods.

'I'd run you up there, but my car's full of cases of wine I've just bought.'

'It's all right, I don't mind walking. See you later.'

Romily escaped into the garden, running down the gravel path between the dripping hedgerows, down through the kissing-gate to the lake and along its edge until she came to the pine trees. James was waiting for her in their shelter and gave her no time to speak, grabbing her up into his arms and kissing her with almost violent greed, making up for the whole week apart. He pushed the hood of her mac off her hair so that he could hold her head in his hands, her mouth a willing prisoner under his. But then his impatient hands were at her belt, undoing it and pulling off her mac. She gasped as she realised what he was going to do, but didn't fight him as he dropped it on the ground and began to

undo her blouse. That, too, he pulled off, but she
had to protest when his fingers went to the catch on
her bra.

'James, you can't! Not here. Not in broad
daylight.'

But he ignored her. 'Why the hell do you bother to
wear this?' he complained thickly. 'It's a pure waste
of time.' His eyes went to her breasts, standing
proud with the firmness of youth. 'And you most
certainly don't need it.' He thrust her bra in his
pocket out of the way and put his hands on her
waist. 'God, I've missed you,' he said fiercely, his
jaw hardening.

A few drops of rain trickled down from the trees
above them, but the rain was warm and not
unpleasant. One landed on Romily's shoulder near
her neck, and rolled slowly down, hovering on her
collarbone for a second and then going on down the
length of her breast. When it reached her nipple it
hung suspended like a bright, shimmering jewel, a
diamond that was reluctant to leave the beauty it
enhanced. James gave a groaning sigh of wonder
and bent his head to take the iridescent drop gently
into his mouth, on to his tongue, and hold it there
until it dissolved and became one with his own
body's moisture.

Romily gazed at him as he lifted his head, her
eyes wide and staring, her mouth parted in deep,
sensuous awareness. 'James.' She whispered his
name and lifted her hands to begin slowly to take off
his clothes. It was the first time she had ever done
so; the first time that she had needed him as much
as he wanted her. When he was stripped to the waist
she raised her hands and slowly explored him, her
fingers running lightly over his skin, touching his

muscles and running through the mat of blond hairs
on his chest. She had never done so of her own
volition before, and the wonder of it was almost
more than he could bear. His hands trembling,
James pulled her slowly towards him so that they
touched, their bodies quivering with anticipation
and desire, his own nipples as hard and aroused as
hers.

'Romily, darling. Sweetheart!' He bent to kiss her
lingeringly, then pulled her head against his chest so
that she could kiss and caress him. Raindrops fell
on them unheeded as they kissed and touched,
Romily giving now as she had only accepted before.
She bit his ear as he nuzzled her neck and moved
her chest against his, loving the softness of his hairs
against her skin, enjoying the strength in his hard
muscles and the width of his broad chest. Her hair
began to cling damply to her head and she pushed it
out of the way with an impatient hand. She was
seized with a sudden hunger and dug her nails into
him, biting at his shoulder as he held her body hard
against him.

'Romily?' He said her name on a thick, demand-
ing note and she knew immediately what he
wanted.

For a moment she buried her face against his
chest, her heart jumping crazily, almost unable to
breathe, then she looked at him, her mouth
trembling, and it was long seconds before she could
breathe, 'Yes!'

A great light of triumph flared in James's eyes
and his hands tightened, hurting her for a moment
before they went to the fastening of her jeans. He
undressed her very slowly, savouring every moment, every curve and shadow that was revealed to

his hungry eyes. He touched her gently, caressingly, passion held achingly in check until there was nothing left to take off. Then he stood up, reached for her hands and put them on his belt.

Her hands trembling, Romily fumblingly began to take off the rest of his clothes, but she was aware always of his eyes on her, dark with need, and the knowledge that they would soon be lovers. It was impossible, too, to ignore the fact that he wanted her very, very badly. Her hands faltered, and James suddenly couldn't wait any longer and lost control. Picking her up, he laid her on their discarded clothes, then tore off the last of his as he lay down beside her. He began to kiss her in wild, deep abandonment, his mouth and hands rousing her into a frenzy of hunger for fulfilment. Her body arched to meet him, desperate to fill the void of emptiness, and he took her in a blaze of passion, their moans lost beneath the sound of the rain.

Afterwards, Romily lay quivering in James's arms, feeling the hammering of his heart, but gradually this, and his ragged breathing, returned to something approaching normal and he raised his head to look at her. His blue eyes were tender, happy, as he kissed her lightly on the corner of her mouth. He smiled, not speaking, and gently traced the outline of her profile with his fingertip, then pushed the wet strands of hair back from her face. She was sheltered from the rain as she lay under him, but could look up at the trees and see the clouds far above. Never again, she thought, would she look up at the rain and not remember that moment.

James's hand moved to her breast and down the long length of her body, stroking her possessively.

She felt him begin to harden as he moved against her and her eyes widened. He smiled down at her. 'I've been waiting for today for a hell of a long time,' he said in soft, unnecessary explanation.

He made love to her more slowly this time, using his body to please and excite her, his experience to lift her close to ecstasy for a moment and then away, prolonging the act of love until she lay writhing beneath him, begging him to love her, love her, love her! And only then did he carry her to the very heights of hedonistic sensuousness, holding back his own climax until he knew that they could share the long waves of pleasure that engulfed them.

It was some time before they dressed, putting their clothes back on anyhow, and walked slowly through the woods to the boathouse. There, James had champagne and caviare already waiting, and Romily looked at him in questioning surprise. 'But how did you . . .'

He shook his head. 'I didn't. This was because we'd been apart for a week, and also because I can never take you out to dinner in the evenings, so I thought I'd bring dinner to you. But as it turns out . . .' Turning her round, he kissed her lingeringly. 'You're wonderful,' he murmured. 'I'd rather eat you than the caviare.'

Laughing happily, Romily pushed him away. 'I must get dry first. Can I borrow your sweater again?'

'Of course.' He got it out of the drawer and gave it to her.

Taking off her outer clothes, she dried herself and pulled the sweater over her head, keeping only her panties on underneath. As she did so, she paused and said, 'Just who *did* knit this sweater for you?'

James laughed delightedly. 'I wondered when you'd get round to asking me that. It was Maggie; she made it for me two Christmases ago.'

'Maggie! And all the time I thought . . .'

He grinned mockingly. 'Don't tell me you were jealous?'

'Certainly not!' But she smiled and came to put her arms round him. James had put on a pair of dry jeans but hadn't yet got round to putting on a shirt. 'Let's open the champagne,' he suggested.

They drank it with the caviare, then opened another bottle and lay back side by side on the big settee, their bare feet entwined, which Romily found very sexy. 'This is like a harem couch,' she said teasingly. 'I bet you bring all your women here.'

James grinned. 'Want to try it out?'

She tilted her head to consider it. 'Possibly.'

'Oh—oh!' He immediately reached for her, but she pushed him away.

'Down, boy! I only said possibly. I haven't finished my champagne.'

'Tyrant,' he grumbled, kissing her throat. 'Do you know you have the loveliest legs I've ever seen?'

Romily lifted one up to inspect it. 'Really?'

'Really.' He slid his hand along her leg. 'All the way from your toes right up to here,' he demonstrated.

Rather breathlessly she put her leg down. 'You're a leg man, huh?'

'Definitely. And any other bits you'd like to display.'

She laughed, looking up at him happily, all her uncertainty gone now as if it had never been. She had committed herself to him and felt secure in her trust. 'James,' she said slowly.

'Mm?' He took a swallow of his champagne.

'You remember you asked me once who had hurt me? What he'd done to me?'

She felt him stiffen beside her. 'Yes.' He put his glass on the floor and turned to face her, giving her his whole attention.

'It was a man who was a guest at the hotel where I worked. He used to stay there often when he came to London on business. He was an executive director with a big firm. He didn't work his way up, he got into it through his family, so he was quite young, only twenty-eight when I met him.'

'How *did* you meet him? You said you never saw the guests.'

'Quite by accident. The staff weren't allowed to use the front entrance, but I'd arranged to meet a friend and I was late, so I ran round to the front of the hotel. We both made a dive for the same taxi and he suggested we share it as we were both going in the same direction. And it—it grew from there.'

'So you had an affair with him?' James said rather heavily.

'Eventually. After about six months. There was no excuse, really. I wanted it as much as he did. But I didn't until he—he bought me a ring. He said it wasn't an engagement ring, but he was always saying what we would do in the future when his job was secure, and I suppose I wanted it so much that I took it that we were engaged. So—I let him take me up to his room.' She stopped, belatedly realising that she had let James make love to her without even mention of marriage or the future, and went on hurriedly, 'It went on for two years, and in the end everyone in the hotel knew about it. They all accepted that we would eventually get married, and even the managers turned a blind eye.' She paused, then said, her voice like lead, 'Which is why it hurt so much when I found out that he was already married.'

'How did you find out?' James asked evenly.

She gave a short laugh, bitter with remembered pain. 'Quite simply. His wife had a baby and they put the announcement in the births column of the Daily Telegraph. A dozen people must have pointed it out to me. And it wasn't even his first child!' She took a long swallow of the champagne, her eyes tight closed.

'So you told him to go to hell, I hope.'

'Yes. Yes, I did.' Romily paused, her voice for a moment too choked to speak, then managed on a gulp, 'But he said—he said he'd grown tired of me anyway. That I'd become—repetitive.'

James swore savagely and held her close to him as she began to shake with sobs, then he started to kiss her eyes, her throat, her lips, until he had driven out the past with the forceful passion of the present and she forgot Richard completely in his arms.

CHAPTER SIX

IT was still raining when James walked back with Romily to the edge of the woods. Taking her in his arms, he held her in a last embrace, and even with all their waterproofs on it still felt good to be held close to him. They had already arranged to meet again in two days' time, but now James looked at her earnestly and said, 'Promise me you'll tell them about us now.'

'Yes, all right.' She smiled at him. 'As a matter of fact Carol and Gerald are giving a party next Sunday—a sort of hotel-warming—and they've said I can bring someone, if I like. Would you like to come to that?'

To her surprise, James hesitated for a long moment before answering, then he nodded decisively. 'Yes, I'd like to.'

They parted reluctantly and Romily ran the rest of the way on a cloud nine dream, telling herself how stupid she'd been not to trust James before. He was a fantastic lover—far better than Richard had been; a thought that made her realise that she was completely over Richard at last. It had been a hurtful and bitter thing to happen, but now she could put it behind her, chalk it up to experience and be glad that she had at least found out the truth and broken with Richard, otherwise she might have gone on waiting for him indefinitely, letting him use her whenever he was in town. But now she had James and the future was suddenly bright and golden again.

She was late getting back and went straight into the kitchen to get on with making dinner. Gerald had not only finished and let another room, but had also taken a booking for a table for four from some people from Inverness who had heard that the food was good here, so there would be fourteen people in to dinner. There was a choice of starter, soup, a set main course, then the dessert trolley, followed by cheese and biscuits, and coffee which could be taken in the lounge on one of the settees in front of the log fire. They had got into the routine of Gerald serving pre-dinner drinks, taking the orders and serving the wine, while Carol waited at the tables and Romily did everything in the kitchen, having prepared as much beforehand as she possibly could with Carol's help. This system had worked all right up to now, but Romily decided they would have to have some extra help soon, especially as Gerald had almost finished decorating two more rooms and didn't anticipate any difficulty in letting them out.

He came into the kitchen shortly after she got back and Romily turned to mention this to him, but something in his face held her tongue. Rather curtly he said, 'You were late getting back.'

'Yes, I know. I'm sorry, but I prepared quite a lot . . .'

But Gerald went on, 'I thought you must still be at Mrs MacPherson's house, so I drove up there to save you the walk in the rain. She said you weren't there, that you hadn't been there.' He pursed his lips angrily. 'So I thought that perhaps you'd gone to meet Ian MacPherson, but his grandmother said that he was at home with a heavy cold and hadn't been out of the house all day. So just where have you been, Romily?'

She groaned inwardly. Why had Gerald had to catch her out today of all days? 'Out,' she prevaricated, playing for time.

'I know you've been out,' he exclaimed. 'What I want to know is where. And who with?'

Guilt made her feel angry herself and she retorted with, 'I'm not a child, Gerald, I don't have to answer to you for what I do in my spare time! If I were just an employee you wouldn't dare ask me such a question.'

He looked taken aback. 'You're my sister. What you do concerns me.'

'It didn't concern you very much before I came to work for you,' she pointed out sharply. 'When you were in Bahrain you hardly even bothered to write!'

Gerald glared at her frustratedly. 'I don't care who you go out with just so long as it isn't Gordon.'

For a minute it didn't register and Romily looked blank. 'Gordon who?'

His grim face relaxed. 'I meant James Gordon. For a minute I thought there might be a possibility that you'd seen him again. But that couldn't be, of course. I'm sorry.' She didn't answer, just looked at him expectantly, and he went on, 'I wouldn't want you ever to go near that swine, Romily.'

'Swine?' she questioned, trying not to show any emotion in her face. 'That's rather a strong word, surely?'

'Not for him,' her brother said with a venom she'd never seen him show before. 'Not for him. Just keep away from him, Romily. Don't go anywhere near him!'

He went away and she let out a long, stunned breath. What on earth had James done to Gerald to make him so angry? But whatever it was must have happened years ago, because she was certain they hadn't met since Carol and Gerald had returned to Scotland. And where did it leave her? She had almost been on the point of telling Gerald when he'd come out with his tirade against James. So now what did she do? She had James making her promise to tell Gerald, and Gerald telling her to keep well away from him. One thing was certain, though; she couldn't possibly let James come to the party now, and she would have to think of some way of trying to break it to Gerald gently. Perhaps if she explained to Carol her sister-in-law might reveal the mystery and help her to bring Gerald round. But if it came to a choice between Gerald's anger and continuing to see James, then she knew James would win every time. If necessary she would leave and Gerald would have to find a new cook, much as she was enjoying her work and didn't want to let him down.

So it was with a mixture of blissful happiness and rather annoyed puzzlement that Romily waited to see James again. She didn't like the feeling that she was deceiving her relations and had made up her mind to ask him what it was all about, at the moment she felt as if she was playing pig-in-the-middle with an invisible ball. But when she came down to make the breakfasts two mornings later she found a hand-delivered letter from James waiting for her on the mat. It read: 'Forgive me, sweetheart, but I can't meet you today after all. I'm mad as hell about it, but business has raised its ugly head and I have to go to London. I'll see you at the party on Sunday. Until then, my darling, my thoughts will be filled with the most wonderful memories. James.'

'Oh hell!' Romily spoke aloud, her disappointment acute. She felt that she had just been living for today, and now she would have to wait until Sunday to see him. No, longer than that because she must put him off coming to the party. She sighed in exasperation. And in frustration; already her body was aching to be loved again. The last line of his letter brought an answering smile to her lips; her thoughts had been filled with very little else, too.

That afternoon she had to be content with going up to Maggie's for another lesson, but first dropped a letter in at the castle for James, telling him not to come to the party and asking him to telephone her so that she could explain. Ian was still at home, but he was much better and hung around until Maggie got fed up with him being under her feet and ordered him back into the sitting-room. He insisted, though, on walking her home, so Romily took the opportunity to let him know, very tactfully, that she would be happy to have him as a friend and neighbour but nothing more. He took it philosophically enough and, it turned out, had been quite expecting her to say it.

'My grandma warned me ye weren't interested in me. I suppose you like the city types?'

'I don't know about city types, but I do prefer— well, older men.'

He laughed. 'I'd better find myself a teenager, then. Maybe to her I'll be an older man!'

She smiled, glad that he was taking it so well. 'We've got a new girl starting at the hotel soon. Come in and have a cup of tea one morning and meet her.'

'Aye, I will.' He walked her right up to the main door. 'Goodbye to you, now.'

'Bye.' he turned to go in just as Carol came to the door, so she left the two of them talking about the garden while she went up to change.

The weather began to improve at last and that weekend was dry and sunny, which Romily thought a shame when she had to stay in and prepare all the food for the party. They had decided to close the kitchen on that day and give the guests the option of going out to dinner or going to the party, and the three couples who happened to be there that evening, all Americans, opted for the party.

When the Sunday morning came round, though, and James hadn't phoned her, Romily began to get a little worried and rang through to the castle to make sure he'd got her message. But the phone was answered by his servant, who said that James wasn't at home.

'He has arrived back from London, though, hasn't he?' she asked anxiously. 'You did give him my letter?'

'Yes, miss. I gave it to him on Friday evening as soon as he arrived.'

'Oh. That—that's all right, then. Thank you.'

She put the phone down, relieved that he'd got her message. Maybe he hadn't thought it worth phoning for an explanation. Maybe he had already guessed why. Which was more than she had done, Romily thought with some annoyance. It had been five days now since she had been with him and she longed to see him again. Just to be near him and touch hands, to look into each other's eyes with the secret knowledge that they were lovers. But now she would have to wait until she could phone him tomorrow and they could arrange to meet again.

All that afternoon she and Carol were busy with

the last-minute preparations, making canapés, arranging flowers, polishing glasses, getting as much prepared as possible of the hot dishes they would be serving for supper. All the feverish rush of things that build up to the excited, urgent feeling that you ought to have when you give a party. By six-thirty they'd done as much as they possibly could and went upstairs to bathe and change, Carol in happy anticipation, but Romily with a dead feeling of anticlimax; without James here as her guest the party loomed ahead very dull and lifeless.

At eight o'clock the three of them gathered in the bar for a much-needed drink before the first of the guests arrived. Carol looked good in a new dress of soft blue silk and Romily had put on a rather sexy black outfit of harem trousers and a top with a very low-cut, swathed back and wide gold belt to match her gold high-heeled sandals. But she rather thought it was going to be lost on her brother's friends. Carol had hired a local girl, Susan, to help on the tables and she had come along tonight to open the door to the guests and take their coats so that Carol and Gerald would be free to serve drinks and circulate while Romily took round the canapés and did all the final food preparation.

The first of the guests arrived promptly at eight-thirty and from then on they arrived in a steady stream. They were nearly all married couples, with here and there an odd divorcee or bachelor who tended to steer well clear of each other until they'd had a few drinks. Romily was introduced to them all, but felt as if she was in a different generation. And as everyone already knew each other, they had lots of friends and interests in common, so that she definitely felt left out of the conversation, too. She began to wonder if, after she had served supper and cleared up, she could sneak away and go up to the castle to see James. This thought made her feel much happier and she quite cheerfully picked up a tray of canapés and began handing them round.

She was standing with her back to the door, exchanging pleasantries with a group of people through the general hubbub of conversation, when the noise level seemed to suddenly drop and she saw the eyes of the couple in front of her widen incredulously as they looked past her. 'My God!' one of them exclaimed, and Romily turned in surprise to see what had created the sudden tension in the room.

James was standing inside the door, one hand still on the knob, the other with the thumb hooked nonchalantly on the pocket of the dark, extremely well-cut suit he was wearing. He looked very handsome, very sexy, and very self-assured. Beside him, every other man in the room became just a member of the masculine gender, but James had it all, and Romily had never been aware of his attraction more strongly than when he stood in the doorway, looking round for her in the ever-growing silence. Her heart seemed to grow in her chest until she found it difficult to breathe and she gazed at him with loving pride. In that moment she knew that she loved him utterly and that the feelings she had had for Richard were nothing compared to this. This was love. This was for always.

It wasn't until after he'd seen her and their eyes had met and held for a long moment that Romily realised that everyone else was staring at him too, and that the silence was one of shocked surprise. Out of the corner of her eye she saw Gerald's face

growing purple with rage and she hastily thrust her
tray into someone's hand just as her brother began
to take a hasty step forward. Quickly she ran up to
James and took his arm, saying loudly, 'So you
managed to make it after all. I'm so glad. Would you
like a drink?' Gerald had come to a dumbfounded
stop a couple of feet away and she turned to him
with a smile, her arm still linked with James's.
'Gerald, I think you already know James, don't
you? From when you were living here before.'

A kind of shocked gasp went up from almost
everybody in the room and Gerald's face went from
purple to white, although Romily didn't know what
on earth she'd said to cause it. Trying to retrieve the
situation, she said hastily, 'He lives up at the castle
on the hill.'

Gerald was so angry that it didn't seem as if he
could answer and she looked desperately over to
Carol for help, but her sister-in-law was just
standing there, her eyes wide in a set face as she
stared at James, almost as if she'd seen a ghost. The
situation was becoming nasty, and what would have
happened if one of their American hotel guests
hadn't stepped forward at that moment, Romily
hated to think. The American woman, obviously
quite unaware of the tense atmosphere, came up
and said to James, 'Did I hear right? Do you really
live in that lovely castle up on the hill?'

James nodded and turned politely to answer her.
There was a sudden flurry of excited comment and
Gerald turned and strode out of the room. Romily
watched him go past, his face set into an icy mask of
rage, his eyes fixed straight ahead, not even
glancing at them as he passed. Feeling suddenly
helpless, she looked again at Carol, but she had

turned and was talking animatedly to the people
near her as if nothing whatever had happened. Her
feelings were in a turmoil of bewilderment, but
Romily just knew that she must stay by James's
side. Whatever the reason for this violent reaction
to his appearance at the party, she must let everyone
know that he was her guest, that she was with him.
So as soon as he'd finished talking to the hotel guest,
she took him out to the bar and got him a drink. He
nodded and said hello to several people as they
walked through the room, so it was evident that
they knew him and were on reasonably good terms
with him. But Romily couldn't help noticing that
nearly everyone kept looking at them, some
surreptitiously, some in open speculation.

They moved to a quieter corner of the bar and
James clinked his glass against hers, his eyes
smiling down at her with just the look she'd hoped
to see there. 'You look very lovely,' he said softly.

But somehow nothing was the same any more
and she said stiffly, 'Didn't you get my message? I
asked you not to come tonight.'

'Yes, I got it.'

'Then why ...?'

But James countered her question with another.
'Why didn't you tell them about us?'

Romily looked down at her drink. 'I was going to
but Gerald found out I hadn't been to Maggie's
that—that last time and asked me if I'd been seeing
you. He got so worked up about it that I—well, I
thought it better not to tell him until I'd talked to
you and found out why he was so against you. Only
you couldn't make Thursday and then you didn't
ring. So I still ...'

She broke off as some newcomers came up to the

bar and went to get their drinks. The man looked round, saw James and said, 'Good God, never expected to see you here, James. Thought this was a no-go area for you since your bust-up with our host and hostess.'

'What bust-up?' his wife asked curiously.

'Oh, it all happened before I met you, darling. Years ago. James, here . . .'

'As you said,' James interrupted calmly, 'it was a very long time ago. And I'm here this evening as Romily's guest.'

He gestured towards her and she gave the couple a tight smile.

'Romily?' the woman repeated. 'Aren't you Gerald's sister?'

'Yes, that's right.' But as she acknowledged it, Romily's eyes moved to the husband, who was giving James a rather stunned look. Then he put a firm hand under his wife's elbow and led her back into the other room, where he began talking to her earnestly.

Romily watched them go, then turned to look at James, her eyes troubled. 'I think you'd better tell me just what's going on. Everyone else seems to know but me.'

He nodded frowningly, 'Yes, I suppose I should have told you before, but I didn't want to spoil things. And I wanted you to hear it first from either Carol or your brother.' He started to say something else but was interrupted by a group of people who came up to have their glasses replenished, and she was kept busy for quite some while.

Gerald came back into the room, his colour more or less back to normal, although he still looked a bit pale. Coming over to her at the bar, he picked up a couple of bottles of wine, opened them and walked back into the main lounge, filling up people's glasses as he went. Romily watched him, feeling slightly sick, her brother had neither spoken to nor looked at her, even though she had been standing right next to him.

As soon as she could, she joined James again. He was talking to some other guests, but broke off what he was saying to smile at her and put a possessive arm round her waist. She had already met the other guests earlier and they had greeted her pleasantly enough, but now they looked at her with a kind of curious fascination, making Romily feel as if her mascara was smudged or her dress was falling off or something. They made her feel uncomfortable and it was a relief when they moved on.

She turned to James fiercely. 'What the hell is it? I feel like a freak the way everyone keeps staring at us.'

His mouth tightening, James said, 'I can't tell you here. Is there somewhere where we can go and talk?'

Doubtfully, she said, 'There's only my room. But I'm supposed to be helping with the party. Carol will want me to serve the food soon.'

'Surely you can take——' He broke off, his eyes on someone behind her. Romily turned and saw that Carol had come into the bar and was looking round. Putting his hands on her shoulders, James turned Romily to face him and said in a low, urgent tone, 'Darling, there isn't time to explain now, but will you please promise me something? Will you please trust me? No matter what Carol or Gerald tell you tonight, will you please remember what we have and trust me?'

Suddenly frightened, she said, 'Why? What is it? I don't understand.'

'Trust me,' he said in a fierce undertone.

Carol came up to them then, her face wearing the sociably charming smile that didn't reach her eyes that she usually reserved for the hotel guests. 'There you are, Romily. It's gone nine-thirty, I've been looking for you to help serve the food.' She turned her head and looked directly at James for the first time. 'Hello, James.'

He nodded shortly. 'Carol.'

'How nice to see you again. I do hope you're keeping well.' Carol went into the second round of social politeness, but her voice was chilling.

But James didn't go on the way he should. Instead of echoing the polite enquiry he put his arm round Romily's waist and drew her close to his side. 'Thank you,' he answered. 'I couldn't be better.' And he deliberately bent to kiss Romily's neck.

Carol's eyelids flickered and her face tightened, but that was all. Whatever emotions she might be feeling were held well under control.

His kiss made Romily angry; she felt as if she was being used by him to make some sort of show of defiance. And she didn't know why, that was the most annoying part. Whatever James and Gerald had rowed about in the past, presumably Carol was all on Gerald's side and must be angry on his behalf. And rightly so. It wasn't—wasn't *gentlemanly* of James to provoke her like this. And Carol was his hostess even if she hadn't personally invited him. Stepping away from James, she shot him a reproachful look and said, 'I—I'll go and do the food now.'

She hurried from the room without looking back,

but was aware again of people breaking off their conversations to look at her, and then looking back at James and Carol.

In the kitchen, she took the big copper pan of deviled beef that had been gently simmering and carried it into the dining-room, then went back for the hot garlic bread and the rice. As she arranged the bread in a basket, Gerald came in, a half empty wine-bottle in his hand. Coming up to her, he caught her arm and swung her round, making her drop a piece of the bread on the floor.

'What the bloody hell do you mean by it?' he exploded. 'I told you to keep away from that filthy swine and yet you have the God-damned nerve to bring him here. Here, to my own house! My own sister, of all people!'

He was shaking her furiously as he spoke, his hands biting into her flesh, his teeth drawn back in a snarl of rage, like a fierce dog.

'Gerald, don't, please. I don't understand. Why are you so angry? What has James done to you?'

He stopped shaking her to stare into her face. 'You mean you don't know? He hasn't told you?'

'Told me what? No, I don't know anything.'

'My God, he's used you, then. Used you to get back into this house. The bastard!' Gerald raged furiously.

He turned to storm into the lounge, but Romily caught hold of him, afraid that he would make a scene, and so frustratedly angry now that she could assert her own will. 'No, you don't! You're not going anywhere until you explain what the hell you're talking about. How has James used me?

What is it I don't know about him? Why don't you like him?'

Her brother's mouth set into a bitter line. 'Ten years ago that—that bastard had an affair with Carol. He seduced my wife! That's why we left here and went to Bahrain. That's why I don't damn well like him!'

Romily stared at him appalled. 'Oh, no! With Carol? But—but she . . .' Her voice trailed away, words failing her. No wonder there had been that deathly hush when James had walked in the room! If everyone had known about it, they must have all been agog to see how the participants in this eternal triangle would react. Only it hadn't been just a trio, she thought on a spurt of anger; she was part of it too now. Only no one had seen fit to tell her.

'I wish I could hit him!' Gerald was fuming. 'I'd like to crush him into the ground! But with all these people here . . . Damn him, the clever bastard. He knew I wouldn't be able to do anything with everyone here. If he lays a finger on Carol, I'll . . .'

'Oh, for heaven's sake,' Romily interrupted him angrily. 'Let's face it, he's in far better condition than you are. If it came to a fight, *you*'d be the one who ended up on the ground. Now, let's get the rest of this food into the dining-room before it goes cold.'

Picking up the tray of garlic bread, she hurried past him, determined to try and play it down so that Gerald wouldn't start a fight or something equally stupid. She didn't know her brother well enough to know if he got drunk easily or not, or how much he'd had already tonight, but anyone could see that it wouldn't take much to push him over the edge into resentful violence. And all over something that happened ten years ago! She could see that it must have been a very traumatic thing to happen to them, but for heaven's sake, it was ten years ago!

'The food's ready,' she called, and went back to stand by the table to ladle out the beef while Carol did the rice, the guests helping themselves to all the different side salads they had prepared. As her sister-in-law walked towards her Romily watched her with new eyes, seeing her as a woman instead of just Gerald's wife. She was still slim, still attractive, especially tonight when she had on her new silk dress and her dark hair cut and styled. She looked good now, so what had she looked like ten years ago when she was only—what—twenty-nine or thirty? A flash of jealousy gripped her and Romily's hand tightened on the ladle. But then she was angry with herself; James would only have been twenty-five, and it was more than likely that it had been Carol who had done the seducing, whatever Gerald said or believed. And it took two to make a love affair.

'The food looks marvellous, Romily darling,' Carol said as she came up. She gave Romily a brittle smile which slipped when she looked into her eyes and saw that she knew—knew and condemned.

But there was no time for words, even if Carol had found anything to say to justify herself. The hungry guests came crowding round, exclaiming at the beautifully laid-out table and standing in line so eagerly that you'd think they hadn't eaten in days.

When everyone had been served, and had drifted away to find a chair or the stairs or floor to sit on to eat, Romily found that she wasn't in the least hungry herself so instead carried the serving dishes back into the kitchen. She stood there for a moment in the comparative privacy of the kitchen, the noise of the party just a hum of talk and laughter from across the hall, and felt suddenly so dejected that she could cry. Even though all this had happened long before she'd even met James, it still hurt to think that he'd been Carol's lover. That he'd held Carol in his arms and done all the wonderful things to her that he'd done to herself less than a week ago. Had they been lovers long? she wondered. Had they believed themselves to be in love, or had it just been sex? A fresh pain gripped her as she imagined them being together in the boathouse, where she and James had made love in such frenzied passion. I'll never go there with him again, she thought fiercely. But there was no doubt in her mind that she would go with him again; she loved him and no ten-year-old affair was going to change that, even if it was so close to home. James had begged her to trust him and she intended to do so. She hadn't given herself to him lightly and she wasn't going to let it end because of this.

She sighed, realising that she would have to leave the hotel; she couldn't carry on working for Gerald and Carol in the circumstances. Lifting the dirty saucepans, she put them in the sink and began to fill them with water, but the girl they'd hired to help came in with a stack of dirty plates and volunteered to take over, so Romily left her to it.

She went to look for James but couldn't find him in the dining-room or either of the other rooms. A sudden fear that he and Gerald might be having a fight made her hurry outside. The driveway was full of cars and she turned to run round to the terrace, but Carol's voice behind her made her stop short.

'Romily, I want to talk to you,' Carol commanded.

'I've got to find James and Gerald. They might be having a fight or something.'

'Nonsense! I don't know where James is, but Gerald has gone down to the cellar to get some more wine.' Coming up to her, Carol said angrily, 'Why didn't you tell us you'd invited James tonight? It was a terrible shock seeing him walk in like that!'

'Well, I wasn't to know it was going to be a shock. And anyway, I didn't know he was coming myself.'

'You mean—you *didn't* invite him?' Carol asked in astonishment.

'Well, yes, I did, but then I told him not to.'

'I don't understand you, Romily,' Carol exclaimed impatiently. 'Did you invite him or not?'

'Yes. But then Gerald warned me off him and I realised James wouldn't be welcome, so I wrote him a letter telling him not to come. But he came anyway.'

'Did he?' Carol's voice had changed subtly, but then it hardened again as she said, 'And just how far has it gone between you two? I take it he's the man you've been seeing in Inverness?'

'Yes,' Romily admitted.

'I see. And I suppose you've been to bed with him?' Carol laughed harshly. 'Going to bed with men means nothing to girls like you nowadays—or to him either.'

'On the contrary.' James's voice came out of the darkness and he walked towards them from the terrace. Putting an arm round Romily's shoulders, he said, 'Romily doesn't sleep around, and I,' he paused deliberately, 'I am far more fastidious than I used to be.'

Carol drew her breath in with a hiss, but then said, 'I'd like to talk to James alone, if you don't mind. We have—things to discuss.'

Before she could speak, James's hand tightened on Romily's shoulder and he said brusquely, 'No, we don't. We had nothing to discuss when it finished and there's nothing now. And don't you think you ought to be getting back inside? I'm sure Gerald will soon miss you even if your guests don't.'

Carol gave him a hard look, but suddenly her face seemed to crumple and she exclaimed in a broken voice, 'Oh, James, how could you come here and do this to me after all we meant to each other?' And then she turned and ran towards the house.

The remembered pain of her own broken love affair came back to her and Romily made to move away from him, but James held her back. 'No, don't run away.' He turned her to face him. 'You mustn't believe her, darling. We didn't mean anything to each other. Carol was bored. Gerald was away on business a lot and she was fed up being alone here with just a young child and her old father for company. She felt that her youth was passing and she wanted some excitement, some romance, if you like. So she threw herself at my head.' He shrugged. 'I'm not making any excuses for myself, but I was young, and when an older woman makes it more than clear that she fancies you . . . well, you tend to take advantage of your good luck. Or that's what it seemed like at the time.'

'How did Gerald find out?'

He gave a harsh laugh. 'Carol found it necessary to confess to him.'

'Oh!'

'Quite,' he agreed. 'As she must have known, he

was the jealous type and created a hell of a fuss, so that in no time at all the whole of Inverness knew about it. Looking back,' he said musingly, 'I think that's why she told him. She wanted everyone to know that she was still capable of pulling a younger lover. And I was fool enough to fall for it,' he added with bitter self-mockery.

Romily moved restlessly and walked a little away from him, turning so that she was looking out over the moonlit waters of the lake. 'Where did you—where did you take her?' she asked hollowly.

Coming up behind her, James put his hands on her waist and bent to kiss her neck. 'The boathouse wasn't even built then,' he assured her, and went on kissing down her bare back almost to her waist. 'Carol was just—part of growing up, experience. While you . . .' He turned her round to face him. 'You are everything I've ever wanted. The one girl I've been hoping and longing for all my life. And I've been waiting so long, my darling, so very long.' Bending his head, he took her lips in a long, sensuous kiss, holding her close to his body, his hands gently stroking her back. They kissed in the moonlight, and James only lifted his head when someone opened a window in the house and they heard the blare of music and noise. 'We'd better go in,' he said thickly. 'You're shivering.'

She smiled. 'No, it's not because I'm cold.' She put her arms round his waist and they stood in each other's arms. 'You still haven't told me,' she reminded him. 'Where did you take Carol?'

'To the house on the island.'

She looked at him with startled eyes. 'So *that's* why you wouldn't take me there?'

He nodded. 'And why I seldom go there myself. It

has no pleasant memories for me. Come on, sweetheart, let's go in. I want them all to see I'm with you. That's why I came tonight.'

'Yes, in a minute. But, James, why didn't you tell me about this yourself? Why let me find out this way?'

'If I'd told you at the beginning—would you have gone on seeing me?'

She hesitated, then shook her head doubtfully. 'No, I don't think so.'

'I'm sure you wouldn't. Especially when it was so obvious that you were getting over someone else. And I didn't want to spoil things for us, didn't want you thinking about Carol and me together all the time.'

'But I was bound to find out sooner or later,' Romily objected.

'Yes, but not until we'd really got to know each other and you'd learned to trust me. As you did,' he said with a smile. 'Eventually.'

'But then why did you urge me to tell them about us during these last two or three weeks?'

'To see what reaction they would have. To know what I had to fight against. As it was they merely warned you to stay away from me without telling you why. But you continued to see me against their wishes.'

She lifted her head to look at him, a frown creasing her forehead. 'And? There must be some other reason?'

James gave a rueful laugh. 'I'm beginning to think you're getting to know me too well! When I felt that we were starting to get close, I wanted you to know because—well, because I didn't want you to fall for me on the rebound. I wanted you to be sure that you really . . .'

He hesitated, and Romily softly supplied the words for him. 'Really loved you.'

His arms tightened sharply. 'Yes,' he agreed, that you really loved me. And tonight I think has proved that. It hasn't made any difference, has it?'

'It hurt a bit at first, but it was ten years ago. That's a lifetime. So now . . .' She shrugged and smiled. 'I know you're experienced with women.' She gave a cheeky laugh. 'I'm very pleased to say!'

James laughed delightedly. 'I'm crazy about you.' He bent to kiss her but exclaimed, 'Your face is freezing! Come on, we'll go and dance to get you warm again.'

Romily really was shivering this time and went inside although she would much rather have spent the whole evening alone with him somewhere. But she, too, wanted to show everyone that his old affair was well and truly over and that she was his new love now.

They stayed at each other's side for the rest of the party, either dancing or talking, and the majority of the guests seemed to accept this, some of them even looking at them with envious eyes, but Carol and Gerald were careful to keep well away. Outwardly, the other two appeared to be enjoying themselves, but Romily knew that their party had been spoilt for them and she was sad about that; they had looked forward to it so much. But she supposed James had been right to force the issue; if he hadn't come tonight she might never have told her family about him and she might have insisted that they go on meeting in secret indefinitely. And James was right; theirs was no clandestine affair, they had nothing to be ashamed of. Everyone knew now that they were in love and probably guessed that they were lovers. But that was OK, too. She was proud to be with him, proud to be loved by him. Involuntarily her hand tightened on his as they danced. James looked down and saw the sensuality in her intent eyes and pouting mouth. He smiled knowingly and bent to softly kiss her lips, then drew her close against him. Romily glanced across the room as she rested her head on his shoulder and saw Carol dancing with Gerald. Her sister-in-law shot her a look of pure, venomous hatred, a look of such malice that Romily's happiness seemed to shrivel and die inside her.

CHAPTER SEVEN

LIFTING her head, Romily stopped dancing and said urgently, 'Let's get out of here.'

James gave her a swift, surprised look but immediately nodded. 'All right.' They walked out into the hall and he glanced out of the window. 'It's raining again. I'm afraid I haven't got my car here, otherwise I'd take you back home with me.'

'We can—we can go up to my room, if you like?'

He nodded, his eyes warm, and Romily took his hand to lead him up the stairs. No one saw them go, the hall was empty, and the hotel guests were still downstairs, enjoying the party, oblivious to all the undercurrents and tension.

When they reached her room, James looked round grimly. 'They don't exactly house you in luxury, do they?' he commented. 'And it's freezing in here!'

'The central heating doesn't stretch this far yet. But there's an electric fire and it soon gets warm.' She bent to switch it on and was surprised at the anger in his face when she looked back at him.

'They could at least have put you in a decent room!'

'It's all right, I like it. Gerald and Carol couldn't afford to have everything done at once and they had to concentrate on getting the rooms ready for the guests.' But even as she spoke Romily gave a convulsive shiver of cold.

With an angry exclamation, James pulled the

patchwork quilt off the bed and wrapped it round her shoulders. 'There, that's better.' He kissed the tip of her cold nose. 'I can see I'll just have to keep you warm.'

'Mm, yes, please!'

The only place where they could sit together was on the bed, so James kicked off his shoes and put a pillow against the brass bedstead, then sat on the bed and leaned against it. Still wrapped in the quilt, Romily half lay against him, her head on his shoulder. They kissed a little, but both of them knew that this was neither the time nor the place for love.

'Why did you want to leave the party so suddenly?'

Romily hesitated, but found herself unable to describe the hatred in Carol's face. Instead she said, 'I'd had enough of people. I wanted to be alone with you.'

That earned her a kiss she didn't really deserve but she accepted it greedily anyway.

'You looked so lovely tonight,' murmured James. 'I was so proud to know that you were mine.'

She looked a little rueful. 'I imagine everyone else realised it, too.'

'Do you mind?'

'No, not really. The circumstances were—a little awkward, though, to say the least.'

'I know, and I'm sorry for that. But it's really better this way. There's been a lot of surmising in the neighbourhood ever since Carol and your brother came back to Scotland. They knew I didn't like the idea of a hotel on my doorstep and they wondered if the old scandal would aggravate things. Now they know that I'm definitely no longer interested in Carol, and by coming here tonight I've condoned the presence of the hotel, so maybe the gossips will be still at last.'

It might have killed any gossip in the neighbourhood, but Romily doubted very much that it was over; both Carol's and Gerald's emotions had been too strongly roused for that. Settling herself more comfortably against his shoulder, she said, 'Did you really think that I was only falling for you on the rebound?'

'It was possible. Quite likely, in fact. I had to be careful not to push you into anything before you were ready. I wanted you to be sure you were making a choice, not just turning to the first man who showed you any affection.'

'Affection? Is that what you call it?' Romily teased. 'I would have used a stronger word myself!' She put her head on one side to look up at him consideringly. 'But of course I'm not on the rebound. Although it would probably have helped to be a little insane if I was going to fall for somebody with as many faults as you have.'

James's eyebrows rose. 'Faults, huh?'

'Well, of course, dozens of them,' Romily declared airily.

His arms tightened round her. 'And would you care to enumerate these faults?' he asked in a dangerously silky voice.

She smiled inwardly, enjoying her game. 'Very well. The biggest fault, of course, is that you're so good-looking. It would have been much better if you'd been ugly.'

'Strange, no one has ever pointed that out to me before,' James remarked. 'I'm sure you're right, of course, but the logic of it escapes me for the moment.'

Pretending to be very patient, Romily explained, 'But it's perfectly obvious. Women are always chasing good-looking men, which means that I shall have to be on the lookout all the time to make sure that some predatory woman isn't trying to seduce you when my back's turned. With an ugly man I wouldn't have to bother.'

James shook with laughter, his blue eyes alight. 'I must admit that's a point that hadn't occurred to me before. But it works both ways, you know, my beautiful darling; I shall have to fight to keep other men away from you.'

He kissed her as he said it, his eyes tender. Pulling the quilt over them, he pretended to reach for her under it. Romily's heart skipped a beat, but she was determined not to get serious, so she caught his hand and said, 'Behave yourself, we're having a serious discussion of your faults. And that's another disadvantage—you're so big! I get a terrible crick in my neck when we kiss standing up,' she complained.

'That's easily remedied,' James returned promptly. 'We'll always kiss lying down.'

'But what if we meet in the street?'

'No problem. I'll spread my overcoat on the pavement for us to lie on.'

Unable to keep a straight face any longer, Romily dissolved into laughter. 'You idiot! I can just imagine you doing that in the middle of Inverness High Street!'

They were still laughing when there was a sharp rap on the door and Gerald walked in on them. While they had been lying there they had heard the sound of cars leaving, and the house had been quiet for a little while now, the party over.

Gerald must have heard their voices and known that James was there, although he must have been coming to her room in any case as he couldn't have heard them unless he'd climbed the stair in the turret. He let out an outraged roar and yelled. 'You bastard, Gordon! You're not content with my wife—you have to seduce my sister too!' He took a hasty step towards them and James got quickly to his feet.

'You leave Romily out of this!'

'You swine! You don't give a damn who you hurt. Well, you're not having my sister!'

'Gerald, for heaven's sake!' Romily threw aside the quilt and got to her feet, Gerald's surprise at seeing that she had some clothes on making her even angrier. 'How dare you burst in here like this?'

'Burst in here? Damn it, this is my house, I'll go anywhere I blasted please!'

'It may be your house, but this is *my* room. And if I care to invite someone up to it, then I shall go ahead and do so,' she retorted furiously. 'And will you please stop swearing?'

But Gerald was too angry to care. 'Can't you see what he's doing? He's trying to seduce you the way he seduced Carol. He ruined her life and now he's trying to ruin yours. I warned you to keep away from him. Why didn't you listen to me?' Coming over to her, he grabbed her wrist and began to pull her towards the door.

Romily protested and pulled back, but it was James saying icily, 'Let her go, Bennion,' that made Gerald stop.

He kept hold of her wrist, though, and glared at

his enemy. 'You're not going to ruin Romily too—I won't let you.' Turning to her, he said earnestly, 'Can't you see that he's no good? He isn't serious about you, you know. Whatever he tells you, it's just lies to get you into his bed. And once he's got you there and sated himself of you, he'll just get rid of you like an old glove. *And* he won't stand by you if you get into trouble. He'll ruin you, Romily, just like he did Carol.'

'No, he won't. Please, Gerald, I know you're worried about me, but it's all right, really. I *want* to be with him.'

'You don't know what you're saying.' He turned on James. 'Get out of here! Get out before I call the police and have you thrown out!'

It was obvious that her brother had had more than enough to drink, and Romily's heart sank, but at least he wasn't so drunk that he was deliberately trying to provoke a fight.

But James didn't help at all; he merely drew himself up to his full height and gave Gerald a sardonic look. 'Go ahead. It's you who'll look a fool. Romily told you, she invited me up here.'

Gerald glared at him impotently, then turned his anger on to Romily, the easier target. 'You little slut! Don't you care what happens to you? I suppose you've had sex with him already, the way he was groping you downstairs. But you're not the only one, you know. He's probably been to bed with most of the women who were here tonight. He doesn't care who he goes with as long as it's wearing a skirt!'

He took a hasty pace backwards as James started towards him but Romily quickly stepped in between them. 'Go away, Gerald! Just leave us alone.'

'Leave you alone? So that he can do what he wants to you, here in my house? Why, you slut—you dirty little tramp!'

Things happened too quickly for her to stop them then. James pushed past her and grabbed Gerald by the collar, his right fist clenched above his face. 'You take that back,' he gritted, 'or I'll ram it down your stupid throat!'

'No! James, *please*.' She grabbed his arm and pulled it down, and after a moment James gave Gerald an angry shake and let him go.

'Get your things together, Romily, I'm taking you away from here.'

Romily bit her lip, wanting to go with him, but knowing the kind of scandal it would cause. She shook her head decisively. 'No, I can't—not like this. You'd better go, James. I'll—I'll call you tomorrow.'

'I can't leave you here with him in that state. Come with me, darling.' He put his hands on her shoulders and looked at her persuasively.

'No, I'll be all right, honestly. Please go now.'

He gave her a long look, then shrugged. 'All right, but you must promise to come straight to me if he starts making things unpleasant for you.'

Before she could speak Gerald gave a harsh laugh. 'It will be a damn sight more pleasant for everybody when you've gone!'

Her patience snapping, Romily turned on her brother angrily. 'Gerald, did you call Carol a slut and a tramp when you found out that she'd been unfaithful to you?'

He fell back as if she'd struck him and James took

the opportunity to kiss her quickly and then go, saying only, 'Don't forget. Don't let him bully you.'

With his going, all the belligerance seemed to evaporate out of Gerald. He collapsed on to her bed as if his legs wouldn't hold him any more, and Romily looked at him in exasperation. Poor Gerald! She had an idea he was his own worst enemy. With a sigh, she lifted his arm over her shoulder and hoisted him to his feet. 'Come on, Gerald, let's get you to bed.'

With some difficulty she helped him along to his flat on the floor above and banged loudly on the bedroom door. She didn't see why Carol shouldn't be woken up and have a share in all the trouble Gerald was causing. But her sister-in-law came to the door still with all her make-up on, and wearing only a diaphanous cream nightdress that left just enough to the imagination. She wasn't at all surprised to see Gerald, but she showed both surprise and disappointment when she saw who it was that had brought him. She expected James, Romily realised, that's why she's dolled up like a bride on her wedding night. Or like a mistress waiting for her lover, she thought bitterly.

Carol's face had changed quickly and now she showed wifely concern. 'What happened?'

But there was a hint of eagerness in her tone that proved that her concern for Gerald was false. She wouldn't have minded if the men had had a fight, she would even have taken secret pleasure in having two men fight over her.

Feeling sickened, Romily said shortly, 'Nothing, of course. Why, what do you think happened?' she demanded belligerently.

'How should I know? Has Gerald passed out?'

'No, I haven't,' Gerald answered for himself truculently. 'I'm just tired, that's all. Bloody women! God, I've had enough!' And shaking himself free of Romily's arm, he made his uneven way into the bathroom and shut the door behind him with a slam.

'Lord, I hope he doesn't fall asleep in there,' Romily remarked. 'We'll never get him out.'

Carol shrugged. 'We'll just have to leave him to sleep it off, then.' She turned to face Romily. 'Has James gone?'

Romily nodded shortly. 'Yes.' She turned to go, but Carol closed her bedroom door and came after her. 'Just a moment. I'd like to speak to you.'

Immediately on the defensive, Romily said coldly, 'What about? I'm tired and I want to go to bed.'

Her beautifully shaped eyebrows raised, Carol said, 'I merely wanted to talk to you about tomorrow. Susan was very good, she did most of the washing up and I put away all the food that was left over for you, so all we have to do in the morning is to make sure the cleaners get the dining-room cleared up in time for breakfast. Not that I think many people will be up early for it—all the hotel guests looked as if they had quite a lot to drink themselves.'

'Yes, it was a good party,' Romily agreed stiltedly.

Carol gave an acid laugh. 'It might have been if you hadn't been stupid enough to invite James here without asking us first. But now you've given the whole of Inverness something to gossip about.' Going over to the sideboard, she picked up a packet of cigarettes and lit one. Romily would have liked to leave, but felt that she had to stay in case Carol needed help with Gerald.

Her sister-in-law blew out cigarette smoke and looked at her narrowly. 'I suppose James told you all about it? I suppose he said it meant nothing to him?'

'No,' Romily corrected her. 'It was Gerald who told me. I didn't know anything about it until this evening.'

'The poor darling,' said Carol, presumably referring to Gerald. 'He was terribly upset when it all happened. That's why we had to leave here and go to Bahrain, you know. God, how I hated that place! So hot all the time. I always longed to come back, but it took me ten years before I could persuade Gerald that it would all have blown over and be forgotten. But then you, you little simpleton, you let James charm you into bringing him here to spoil everything for us again. Heaven knows how long it will take Gerald to get over this!'

'James didn't come here to make trouble for you,' Romily retorted, immediately springing to his defence. 'He merely came as my escort.'

Carol gave one of her high-class trills of laughter. 'My dear girl, if you believe that you'll believe anything! Do you really believe that James is in love with you? I doubt if he even fancies you. You're not his type.'

That's what you think! Romily thought fiercely, but aloud she said, 'Well, Gerald doesn't agree with you. He seems to think that James goes for anything in a skirt. He even had the cheek to tell him so.'

'Really?' Carol was immediately diverted. 'What did James do?'

Romily remembered the anger in James's face

but wasn't going to give Carol the satisfaction of knowing. 'Nothing. He realised that Gerald was drunk.'

Carol laughed. 'And also because he knew that it wasn't true. James is a macho kind of man who acquires that kind of reputation just because women can't resist him. But that doesn't mean that he can't resist *them*. He's had women, of course, but there was only one that really meant anything to him.'

My God, she means herself, Romily realised with astonishment. Coldly she said, 'Really? Who was that? Someone you know?'

Carol laughed again, but there was a cutting edge to it this time. 'I mean myself, Romily darling. Do you really think I would have risked my marriage like that if James and I hadn't fallen desperately in love? We tried to fight against it, of course, or at least I did, but I'm afraid James went all out to win me. He just couldn't wait to make love to me.'

Romily turned away, unable to look at the other woman. 'For heaven's sake, Carol! You're writing your own scenario. Or have you come to believe that it happened like that because that was the way you wish it really happened?'

Getting to her feet. Carol said petulantly, 'That *is* the way it was. We were crazy about each other.'

'But you were five years older than he was.'

'Only four.' Carol caught herself up and smiled grimly. 'But the age difference didn't matter. We both knew it was the real thing.'

'So why didn't you stay with him, then, if you were so much in love?' Romily asked sneeringly.

'I would have done—James begged me to often enough. I would have divorced Gerald and married him if it hadn't been for Christopher,' she declared, naming her eldest son. 'I couldn't let him go. He was so young, only two years old. And Gerald refused to give me custody of him. It wasn't so easy ten years ago. It wasn't so simple to get a divorce. And then I still loved Gerald. In an entirely different way, of course. And I didn't want to hurt him.'

'So you conveniently went back to the poor devil when James broke it up,' sneered Romily.

'My dear Romily, what a lot you have to learn about men—and about love. Though I don't expect you have much experience of the latter yet, have you?' Carol said cattily. 'My love affair with James was stormy and tempestuous. We were always on a high plateau of love because we both knew that it couldn't last, that in the end I would go back to my child.'

'And your husband,' Romily pointed out coldly.

'Of course. But James vowed that he would never stop loving me, that he would wait for ever if he had to, in the hope that I would one day be free to marry him.'

'That's ridiculous!' Romily exclaimed. 'No one makes declarations like that. You're just making it up.'

'Am I? I'd only have to lift a finger and James would come running back to me,' boasted Carol.

'Now I know you're lying!' Romily declared triumphantly. 'Because only tonight James asked me to go and live with him.'

Her left eyebrow arching in disbelief, Carol said, 'What do you mean?'

'Exactly what I said. When Gerald started going off at me James offered to take me away from here.'

'To take you away, yes. James was always gallant,

even with people like you. But not, I think, to live
with him.'

Romily was silent, trying to remember his exact
words, but before she could speak Carol said
swiftly, 'I thought not. And I'm quite sure that he
hasn't asked you to marry him. Or even told you
that he loves you. And he won't,' she went on in
gloating triumph, 'because James is a man of his
word, and he gave his promise to me when I had to
leave him ten years ago.'

Romily's chest felt tight, but she clung stubbornly
to her belief in James. 'That isn't the way he tells it.'

'My dear, I didn't think for a moment that he told
you the truth. The memory of it is far too precious
for him to tell anyone, especially to you when he was
only using you so that he could see me again.'

Romily gasped incredulously. 'My God, you
don't seriously believe . . .' She laughed, sure now
that Carol was only saying what she wished was
true. 'Go to bed, Carol, I think you've had as much
to drink as Gerald, only yours has gone straight to
your imagination. I'll see you in the morning.'

She went to walk out of the room, but Carol called
after her angrily, 'If you don't believe me, try asking
James just why we broke up!'

Romily paused for a moment with her hand on
the doorknob, looking back at her sister-in-law's
still attractive face and slim figure. She's a bitch,
she thought. The first real bitch I've ever encoun-
tered, and I didn't even realise it. There were a
dozen remarks she could have made, but she
refused to lose her temper, instead walking silently
out of the room and closing the door quietly behind
her.

For what was left of that night Romily slept only

scrappily, her mind often surfacing to go over the
events of that terrible evening, but she was up at six-
thirty to make sure that the cleaners had finished
with the dining-room in time for her to lay the tables
for breakfast. Carol had been right about the guests
who'd been to the party coming down at the last
minute, and two of the wives didn't appear at all,
but the other people who were staying there all
came down for breakfast as usual, and as neither
Gerald nor Carol put in an appearance Romily had
to do the cooking and serve as well. She didn't really
mind; eight breakfasts were nothing, and she
supposed her relations had some excuse for being
irresponsible today, but she wondered what would
have happened if she had decided to take the
morning off too. Would the guests have had to get
their own breakfast?

When the last guests had left the dining-room
after their usual chat about how they were going to
spend their day, she was able to relax her fixed smile
and hurry to the phone. 'James.'

'Are you all right?' he asked urgently.

'Yes. Yes, I suppose so. Can we meet today?'

'Yes, of course. This afternoon? At the boathouse?'

'All right. I'll be there at two-thirty. James?'

'Yes?'

'Oh, it—doesn't matter. It's nothing.'

'What's wrong, Romily?'

'Like I said, it's nothing. I'll see you this
afternoon. 'Bye!'

She went slowly back to the kitchen and cleared
up after breakfast, then sat down to write a rough
copy of the dinner menu. While she was doing this
Carol came in and Romily stiffened, expecting her

to display some of the nastiness that she'd shown
last night, but Carol was her usual model of
sweetness and light and behaved as if nothing at all
had happened. That suited Romily just fine, and
she was able to concentrate on making the pudding
for the dessert trolley and preparing whatever else
she could for the evening meal. Gerald didn't put in
an appearance until nearly lunchtime and, if
anything, looked worse than he had last night. He
groaned quite a lot, his drunken brashness of
yesterday completely gone, demanded to know
where the Alka-Seltzer was, and then disappeared
again.

All her chores were finished before lunchtime,
but Romily didn't feel like eating with the others, so
she made herself a ham roll and went out in the car,
driving to a quiet spot off one of the valley roads
where she parked and looked out over the mountains, some of them still capped with snow on their
peaks, but beginning to show the brilliant green of
new grass at their feet. She ate her roll and drank a
can of Coke, her eyes on the impressive landscape
but her mind miles away. Try as she might, she
couldn't forget what Carol had said last night.
Especially that last parting shot when she'd told
Romily to ask James why they'd broken up. What
was so mysterious about that? Presumably James
had just got tired of the whole thing and wanted to
end it. Which was bad luck on Carol, of course, if
she was still keen on him, but it was obvious that it
would have to end some time. James had admitted
to Romily that on his part it was just a sexual
experience, whatever Carol thought it. But he
hadn't actually said why it had ended, now that she
came to think about it. He had just said that Carol

had confessed to Gerald and there had been a hell of a fuss. Had she confessed to try and force Gerald into divorcing her and James into doing the decent thing and marrying her? Romily wondered. After last night she wouldn't put that past Carol at all.

Romily sat on in the car, musing, wondering, feeling strangely unsure again until it was time to drive back to meet James. Today she drove straight to the boathouse and found James already there, waiting. As soon as she came up the stairs into the room, he shut the door behind her and took her in his arms. He kissed her avidly, his lips greedy for the response he soon aroused in her.

'James . . .' She tried to speak to him but he wouldn't let her, his mouth devouring hers in a heat of need. His hands went to the buttons of her jacket and he took it off, then to the fastening of her skirt. His hot breath scorched the hollow of her neck as he kissed her throat, her chin, bit hungrily at her ear. 'Oh, James. Oh, God!' She began to take off his clothes too, a button tearing off in her haste, their hands getting in each other's way as they undid buckles and pulled at zips.

James pulled her sweater over her head and gave a glad cry of wonder when he saw that her breasts were bare. 'Oh, sweetheart!'

'You said—you said that bras were a waste of time,' Romily said breathlessly, for already his mouth had found her and she moaned at the sudden ecstasy of it.

He went on kissing down her body as he bent to take off her shoes and tights. 'You're beautiful,' he murmured as he looked up at her. 'Perfect.' He kissed her again, the most intimate kiss she had ever known, driving her body into an aching, screaming need for fulfilment.

She gave a long, shuddering moan and drew away. 'James, please, please love me—I can't take any more!'

Quickly he picked her up and carried her over to the sofa that was as big and soft as a featherbed. He laid her down on it with her head on the arm and stood beside it as she reached up to take off the last of his clothes. With clothes on James was extremely good-looking, without them he was beautiful, his hard body slim and tanned, with long legs and a firm, flat stomach, a narrow waist but broad, strong shoulders. He stood for a moment, letting her look at him, then lay down beside her, his hands stroking her skin, discovering every part of her anew. 'Is this what you like?' he breathed. 'And this?'

'Yes, oh, yes,' she moaned in reply, her body arching to meet his hands.

And when he had had his fill he took her hand and put it on his own body. 'Now you can have your turn,' he said softly.

To touch and caress him was a surfeit of pleasure because it not only aroused James even more but her too. Their breath grew hot and gasping, sweat broke out on James's skin as he strove to control himself until she had explored him as he had her. Her fingers touched in caresses light as a kiss, tantalising, enticing, making him shake with anticipation.

No need to ask what he liked, his body told her that when it quivered as she touched him, and soon his gasping breath had turned to groans.

'Romily. Oh, dear God!' He lay on top of her, his hands buried in the thickness of her hair as he lifted her head to meet his. 'My dearest, my love!'

His rampant body took hers, slowly at first and then with ever-increasing fervour. Waves of heat and pleasure washed over her and she felt as if she was drowning in a bottomless sea of sensuality, sinking deeper and deeper until it engulfed her. Her hot damp skin, the thrust of her breasts and thighs as she responded to the urgency of his lovemaking, drove James to a savage frenzy of passion. He cried out her name over and over again as his body arched in spasm after spasm of climactic excitement.

Romily lay with her head on his shoulder, completely content, slowly floating up from the depths of physical fulfilment through all the layers of pleasure and happiness to the commonplace joy of just being close to him, held in his arms and able with every sense to know that he was there, loving her. Slowly she opened her eyes to see James smiling tenderly down at her. 'I think,' he said softly, stroking her damp hair from her forehead, 'that you enjoyed that.' His heart that had been thundering before now only beat like a loud hammer.

'I think you did too. Just a little.'

'Just a little,' he mocked, 'Did I say hallo to you, by the way?'

'No. Somehow I don't think there was time.'

He chuckled against her hair and gently blew at a strand of it that lay across her cheek. 'I'm crazy about you.'

'Are you?' Romily turned her head to look at him, her eyes suddenly serious.

'Can you doubt that, when we're together like this?' he said softly. 'Oh, Romily, don't lose your trust in me. Not now, not after what we've just shared.'

'No, I haven't. Of course I haven't.' She said it quickly, reassuringly, but then lay still, her eyes turned away and not speaking.

After a few moments James gave a harsh sigh. 'All right, Romily, you'd better tell me. What's happened?'

'Nothing. Only—only last night, after you'd gone, Carol started talking to me.'

He gave a derisive snort. 'She would! And succeeded in planting some poison in your mind, by the sound of it. I should have insisted that you come away with me last night. Right, let's have it. What did she say?'

'All kinds of things. Mostly about the two of you. That you'd been madly in love and that you'd begged her to leave Gerald to marry you. And that . . .'

But she didn't get any further, because James had started to shake with laughter. 'You don't mean to tell me you believed any of that rubbish? All either of us was interested in was sex. If Carol has embroidered it since then I feel sorry for her. But I made it plain from the beginning that I wasn't in love with her and that I had no intention of coming between her and Gerald. But she went and told him.'

'Why? Why did she tell him?'

James hesitated, then lay back on the settee and shrugged. 'At first all she wanted was a sexual adventure too, but then she started to get serious. Maybe she liked my lifestyle, I don't know. I just wanted to be finished with her, but she clung like a vine. When it finally got through to her that I didn't want to know, she resorted to all kinds of threats and finally told Gerald. In the hope that he would have divorced her and I'd have married her, I suppose.'

'And would you have done?'

'My God, no! She was bad news then, and it sounds as if she still is the way she's trying to poison your mind.' James turned to look at her. 'You didn't seriously believe her, did you?'

Romily smiled and put a hand on his still damp chest. 'No. Even the way she told it seemed all wrong. But some things she said she seemed so sure of.'

'Oh? What were they?' Picking up her hand, James began to gently bite her fingers.

'Well, she said that she only had to lift a finger and you would go running back to her.' James made an extremely rude noise against her hand and she burst into laughter. 'So that's what you think of that idea, is it? You're terrible!'

'Most definitely. Do we have to go on talking about Carol? I can think of other things I would much rather do with your mouth.'

'In a minute you shall do exactly as you like with it. But there was one other thing she said, right at the end. She said that if I didn't believe her I should ask you why you broke up. Now, why should she . . .' Her voice trailed off as James's fingers suddenly tightened on hers.

But then he smiled at her and said, 'I told you— she got too clinging.'

'Nothing else?' she asked, slightly puzzled.

'Nothing else at all, my darling. And now I seem to remember that you made a promise concerning your mouth,' he murmured as his hands began to stoke her into awareness. 'And I think we'll start with this . . .'

Romily was more than happy again when she got back to the hotel, her face radiating the fulfilled lovemaking of the afternoon. Hurrying into the kitchen, she found Carol already there, preparing some salad.

'Two of the guests met some friends while they were out and rang to ask if they could bring them back for a meal. So that will be two extra for dinner. Is that all right?'

'Yes, we should have enough. Although we might have to have something different for our own dinner,' Romily answered, her professional mind immediately taking over.

'Oh, good. I've started making the salad. Is there anything else you want me to do?'

'You can coat the fish I prepared this morning with the seasoned flour, if you like.'

Romily took her plastic apron from the drawer to start work, and as she did so Carol gave her a closer look. 'You look very happy. I suppose you've been with him?'

For a moment Romily hesitated, but then realised that there was no point in trying to hide it. 'With James. Yes.'

'And did you ask him why we broke up?'

'Yes, I did as a matter of fact.' Romily took a knife from the rack and began to skilfully cut up some carrots. 'He said that you broke up because you became too serious and clinging. Like a vine, was the way he described it, I believe.'

'Did he really?' Carol retorted with an angry sneer. 'But it seems that he neglected to mention one small detail that led up to it.'

'What was that?' asked Romily with sudden misgiving.

Glaring at her, Carol said scathingly, 'Only that he happens to be the father of my younger child!'

CHAPTER EIGHT

ROMILY stood very still for a moment, then looked down at the red blood where the knife had sliced into her hand. Dropping the knife, she went quickly into the little cloakroom opening off the kitchen, closed the door behind her and plunged her hand under the cold tap.

'Romily? Romily, are you all right? Is it a bad cut?'

Carol's voice came from the other side of the door but for a moment Romily couldn't bring herself to answer. But when Carol called out again she somehow cleared the lump from her throat and said loudly, 'Yes, I'm all right.' She cleaned the cut carefully and put on a Band Aid, noting almost absentmindedly that it wasn't too deep. And it didn't hurt at all. But she probably wouldn't have felt it even if it had hurt, right now she felt almost completely numb with shock.

It took considerable courage to walk back into the kitchen with her head held high, her face impassive, and maybe she didn't fool Carol at all, but it certainly helped. Picking up the knife again, she washed it and went on slicing the carrots. Carol gave her a long look, then she, too, gave her attention to preparing the dinner. But when at last Carol went upstairs to get changed, Romily slumped against the table, the strength that had carried her through the last hour suddenly draining

away. A dozen thoughts and pictures that she'd
resolutely pushed out of her mind came flooding
back. Carol's youngest son, Simon, was nearly ten
years old, the right age, and he had fair hair. But his
eyes weren't blue, he had Carol's hazel eyes. But
then she remembered James asking about Simon
when they'd first met, how he'd remembered his
name, although he hadn't asked about Christopher.
She sat down in a chair, trembling. It couldn't be
true, it couldn't possibly. But even Carol wouldn't
have made up something like that. And it would
account for all the amazement when James had
walked into the room at the party, and the terrible
hatred that Gerald still had for him after all these
years. No wonder they had gone to Bahrain! No
wonder that little Simon had been sent to boarding-
school just as soon as he was old enough. The poor
kid was a constant living reminder to Gerald that
his wife had been unfaithful to him.

A pan started to boil and Romily automatically
went over to the cooker to turn down the heat. But
why hadn't James told her when she'd asked him
why they'd broken up? She remembered that he'd
hesitated. Was this why? Had he been on the point
of telling her and then changed his mind? There
could be a dozen reasons for that, she supposed, but
without asking him she would never know.

Carol came down again, looking sophisticated in
a dark skirt and sweater and Gerald soon followed
her, wearing his usual wine-coloured velvet jacket
and looking more himself but still rather taciturn.
As usual, they all became rapidly busy as the guests
came down and made their choices from the menu.
Romily worked as efficiently as always, but tonight

she was silent, unable to find anything to say in answer to Gerald's grumbles about people not being able to make up their minds, or Carol's comments on the guests' clothes.

When dinner was over at about nine-thirty, they usually had a late meal themselves, eating in the kitchen, but tonight Romily only laid places for two.

Glancing at the table, Carol said, 'Aren't you eating with us?'

'No, I'm not hungry. I'll just take a sandwich up to my room and have an early night.'

A sardonically amused look came into Carol's eyes. 'You're not sulking, are you?'

'What should she be sulking about?' demanded Gerald, coming into the room behind her.

'I'm not . . .' Romily's voice rose on a hysterical note, but she bit her lip hard and then spoke more normally. 'I am not sulking. I'm very tired, that's all. If you remember I had to get up early this morning to do the breakfast. *I* didn't just lie in bed until I felt like getting up.'

'Not this morning, no,' Carol said maliciously. Then, putting on one of her charming smiles, 'I'm so sorry, darling, but it *was* rather an exception. Don't worry, we won't leave you to cope on your own again.'

'You won't be able to,' Romily answered clearly. 'Because I'm leaving. You'd better find yourself another cook straight away.'

'But you can't do that!' exclaimed Gerald in horror. 'You'd said you'd stay for at least the first season.'

'So I've changed my mind. I find I don't like it

here any more.' She shot Carol a hostile, challenging look, but the other woman merely sat there with a small, catlike smile on her lips.

She wanted this, Romily thought as she turned to go. She wants me out of the way so that she can try to get James back. Her legs felt leaden as she climbed up the stairs to her room. Four of the guests who had been at the party were standing on the landing, talking, and she had to give them a smile and a pleasant goodnight.

'Do you work here?' one of them asked.

'Yes, in the kitchen. I'm the cook.'

'You are?' the woman exclaimed. 'But you're so young to make all those wonderful things!'

So then Romily had to explain about her previous experience and how she came to be there.

'So you're Mr Bennion's sister. How lucky for him! And was that your boy-friend you were with at the party? The one who owns the castle?'

Romily hesitated for a brief moment, but then her chin came up. 'Yes, that's right,' she declared, 'he's my boy-friend.'

Wow! And do you two plan to get married?'

Immediately she was deflated, not really knowing how James felt about her. 'I—I don't know. We haven't known each other very long, you see. Only two or three months.'

'Leave the young lady alone,' one of the men admonished her questioner. 'Can't you see you're embarrassing her?'

Romily gave him a grateful smile, said a hurried goodnight and escaped to her room at last. She lay on her bed, feeling hungry and wishing that she'd remembered to bring a sandwich, but there was no

way she was going to go back to the kitchen to make
one while Gerald and Carol were there. Her mind
went back to that inquisitive woman on the
landing. The woman's questions had been meant
kindly, of course, she was obviously just interested
in everyone she met, but they had made Romily
look at herself through someone else's eyes. The
questions had been so cut and dried. Is he your
boyfriend? Are you going to marry him? Very
simple to ask, almost impossible to answer. When
she was with James, and especially when they had
been making love that afternoon, she had been
absolutely sure and certain that it was right and that
they loved each other. That they would spend the
rest of their lives together and that there would be
no future without him. But now she made herself
face the fact that James had never once said he
loved her except that time this afternoon when, in
the heights of passion, he had called her his darling,
his love. Had he meant it, or had it just been another
endearment, another word? But there was no
question in her mind about marriage. He had never
mentioned it once.

So what did he want from her? Getting to her
feet, Romily went over and looked at herself in the
mirrors of the old dressing table. Front view, in
profile; she saw a tall, slim and attractive girl with
big eyes in a pretty face and thick, glowing red hair.
The kind of girl that any man would enjoy going to
bed with. But would he want to marry her? Perhaps
she was just the kind that men used and then left,
she thought bitterly. Oh, God, she was so unsure of
herself again, so afraid that she had, for a second

time, given her love to a man who only wanted her body.

Suddenly she turned and smashed her fist against the wall. James wasn't like that, he wasn't! He hadn't rushed or pushed her in any way, had in fact been patient and understanding. OK, so maybe he hadn't told her that he had given Carol a child, but maybe he thought it wasn't his secret to tell. And being with him—well, that was wonderful, wasn't it? So what the hell was she worrying about?

Her brain seething with crazy, mixed-up emotions of anger and fear, Romily at last dropped into an exhausted sleep, but there were dark shadows under her eyes when she got up next morning to make breakfast. To her surprise she found Gerald already in the kitchen making the first preparations. 'Morning, Romily,' he greeted her.

'Hello. You're up early,' she answered listlessly.

'Yes. I—er—wanted to talk to you before Carol came down. Look, you weren't serious last night, were you? About leaving us, I mean?'

'Yes,' she told him baldly. 'I don't want to get involved in your—private affairs.'

'I know that, and I'm sorry. I realise that I didn't behave very well the other night. But it was a shock, you see, seeing him just walk in here as bold as brass like that. It brought back all kinds of memories.'

Romily gave her brother a sympathetic look, realising that he was the one who had suffered most in all this. 'I didn't know James was coming,' she explained. 'When you said you didn't like him I tried to put him off, but he came anyway.'

'Yes, I know—Carol told me. I'm sorry I went off

at you, called you the things I did. I was angry, you
see.'

'I did notice,' she commented drily.

'Come and sit down and have some coffee.' He
put two mugs on the kitchen table and sat opposite
her, reminding Romily of when she'd been very
young and Gerald had been home from university
on holiday, sometimes he had made her breakfast
and they had sat opposite one another like this, he
already a young man, she a tot of five. Maybe
Gerald remembered it too, because he smiled and
said, 'In some ways I feel more like a father to you
than a brother.' He gave a short laugh. 'We're a
couple of innocents in all this, aren't we?'

Romily didn't answer and he looked down at his
mug before saying with difficulty, 'You mustn't
take too much notice of Carol. She slipped just that
once and it ruined her life as far as she was
concerned. She had to give up the position she had
here and I had to give up a really good job, so that
now we're down to this, running around waiting on
tourists. She wasn't meant for this kind of thing,
Romily.'

'Nor were you,' she reminded him. 'It ruined your
life too.'

He shrugged. 'Oh, I don't matter. It doesn't worry
me any more what I work at as long as I can earn a
decent living.' He looked wistful. 'I've missed not
seeing the boys from one year's end to the next,
though.'

Taking a deep breath, Romily said, 'Carol told
me that Simon—isn't your son.'

His eyes grew bleak. 'She told you that, did she?
She shouldn't have done that. It wasn't necessary.'

'Is it true?' she asked urgently.

Gerald looked down at his mug again. 'I don't know,' he admitted, and took a long drink.

'But—but you must *know*!'

He shook his head. 'No, I don't. Either of us could have been the father.'

But surely you must have had blood tests taken to . . .'

'No,' he interrupted her shortly, then looked at her pleadingly. 'Don't you see? If I'd insisted on having tests done I might have found out that Simon—Simon wasn't mine. This way I can go on loving him because there's always the possibility that he is.'

Romily stared at him wide-eyed. 'And go on loving Carol, too,' she added softly.

Gerald nodded and stood up. 'Yes, that too, Romily,' he said looking at her directly, 'please don't leave us unless—unless you feel you absolutely have to. We need you here, and I'd like to think that we have given you some sort of home.' She didn't answer, so putting down his empty mug he said in quite a different tone, 'If you tell me what vegetables you want from the market, I'll go and get them.'

All the time she was working that morning, Romily could think of little else but what Gerald has said. He was right in many ways; both he and she were the innocent victims of an old affair, but even though she sympathised with him, Romily didn't see how she could stay on at Abbot's Craig. She had an idea that even though Carol knew she was cutting her own throat, she would still make life a misery until she got rid of her. Her pride wouldn't allow her to see James with someone in her own house, someone younger and prettier than Carol was. It would remind her always of what she had experienced in James's arms.

So Romily decided she would definitely leave as soon as Gerald found someone to take her place. But where would she go? To James? Up until yesterday that would have been the only thing for her to do, but now . . .? Now she wasn't sure any more, even though he had told her to go to him.

They had arranged to meet at the boathouse again that afternoon and Romily left the house in time to walk there to meet him, but as she went through the garden down to the lake, her footsteps slowed. Instead of walking to the woods, she turned and walked slowly out on to the jetty, repaired and cleaned now since Gerald had bought a small boat with an outboard motor for the use of his fishing guests. Two of them were out in it now, far over on the other side of the lake where the trees hung over the water making dark pools where the fish liked to feed. Someone had left a rod on the jetty, the line baited, and she sat down beside it, waiting to see if she would catch a fish.

It was half an hour before James came to look for her. He was wearing jeans tucked into his boots, and a sweater, his head bare. He stopped at the edge of the wood when he saw her sitting there, and came over to squat down beside her on the jetty. 'Caught anything yet?'

She shook her head, not looking at him. 'No.'

'I thought we had a date.'

'Yes, I know.'

'But you decided not to keep it?' She didn't

answer, just sat looking at the end of her line, so James said grimly, 'All right, Romily, what is it?'

Slowly, painfully, she said, 'Why didn't you tell me that Simon is your son?'

'Because he isn't.'

The answer was so immediate, so assured, that she swung round to stare at him.

'But Carol said . . . She couldn't have made up something like that, James. She just couldn't!'

'No, she didn't, not entirely. There was a possibility that the child could have been mine. But it was unlikely, I'd only been seeing her—under duress, if you like, by then.'

'So you don't actually *know* that he isn't yours?'

'Yes, I do. When she started to use her pregnancy to try to make me marry her, I insisted that a blood test be done as soon as the child was born. It proved conclusively that Simon wasn't mine.' He looked steadily into her eyes. 'Carol decided she wanted to marry me, you see, and what Carol wants she goes all out to get. When I made it plain that I wasn't interested in marriage, or in her any longer, she put on a big act about killing herself if I didn't, said that she was crazily in love with me and all the rest of it. I didn't have much experience of handling that kind of thing then, and she managed to coerce me into having sex with her one last time. Then some weeks later she told me she was pregnant. That the child was mine and that she would have to tell Gerald who would probably kill her,' and would definitely throw her out. It came,' James said grimly, 'as rather a shock. I thought I was well rid of her. She tried, of course, to play on my better nature, but I was beginning to see through Carol by then, and decided that she was probably lying. But she produced a doctor's certificate to prove that she was indeed pregnant. So then I realised that she must have deliberately allowed herself to get pregnant in an attempt to coerce me into marrying her. But I was damned if I was going to have my life ruined because of her,' he finished forcefully.

Romily turned away for a moment, remembering how Gerald's life had been ruined instead, how the weaker man had borne the brunt of all this.

'I decided to call her bluff,' James went on. 'But she went ahead and told Gerald and all her women friends in Inverness. Gerald came up to the castle spitting fire and I let him knock me down a couple of times because I figured I deserved that much for what I'd done to him. But then he completely took the wind out of Carol's sails by vowing to stand by her. When the baby was born she tried to stop me having the blood tests done because she wanted to continue to use the child as a threat. She knew I wouldn't marry her, so she wanted to do me as much harm as possible. But I wasn't going to have that child held as a sword over my head, so I took it to law and she was forced to have the tests done.'

Romily looked at him curiously. 'And if he had been your child? What would you have done?'

A dark look came into his blue eyes. 'Paid for his upkeep, made sure he was all right, cared about him. But I would never have married Carol even if Gerald had divorced her. That woman is vile, poisonous!'

'Maybe she did love you,' Romily said slowly. 'Maybe she loved you so much that she was willing to do anything to keep you.'

James gave her a swift look, then shook his head decisively. 'No, I don't buy that. She fancied me all right, but she was more in love with what I could give her than with me. Catching me would have been good for her ego, that was all. As it was, all she did was to hurt everyone concerned: herself, me, Gerald, and even Simon and her other son in some ways. And now you.'

Romily let that go, but said, 'Did Gerald know that the blood tests were done?'

'I don't know,' answered James with a shrug. 'My solicitors certainly informed Carol of the results, but I left it to her to tell Gerald. Why?'

'She never told him,' said Romily on a disbelieving note. 'He still doesn't know and now he doesn't want to. He's afraid to, I think.' They sat in silence for a few minutes until she asked. 'Why didn't you tell me all this before? When I asked you why you'd broken up with Carol?'

'Because it's all so damn sordid,' he explained vehemently. 'And because it all ought to be forgotten and done with. Having to admit to you that I'd had an affair with Carol was bad enough, but this as well . . .'

She turned away and looked at the rod which had started to quiver. 'But why should you care so much how I feel about it?'

'You know damn well why,' James told her forcefully.

Romily almost cried out that she didn't know, that he had never told her, but instead she said with difficulty, 'Did you ever tell Carol that you loved her?'

He looked away, his mouth set into a grim, bleak

line. 'Yes, probably I did. At the beginning. It was easy to say that to a woman, especially when you were making love to her. They—they expected it. It seemed to make it better for them if they thought it wasn't just sex. Even though they knew that in reality it wasn't true. But since Carol I've never made that mistake again. I've never told a woman that I loved her because it hasn't been true.' He laughed harshly. 'At least I learned that from Carol; not to be dishonest to a woman even if she wants you to lie.'

He turned to say something else to her, but the line began to jerk and she jumped to her feet. 'Oh, I've caught a fish! Quick, what do I do?'

'Don't you know?'

'No. Somebody just left the line here.'

'Here, take it in your left hand and start to reel the fish in with your right.' He came up behind her to put his hands over hers, showing her how to gradually pull the fish into the bank. But the line suddenly went slack and when James lifted it out of the water they saw that it was empty. 'It got away.' James replaced the rod on its stand and turned to her. 'Let's go back to the boathouse,' he said urgently.

Romily shook her head. 'No, I—I don't think so.'

'Why not?'

'I'd like to—think things over.'

His mouth grew grim. 'I thought you cared enough to trust me. Don't tell me you still believe Carol?'

'No, but I ...' Her eyes filled with tears. 'Somehow I feel—dirty!' And then she turned and ran back to the house as James watched her, his eyes bleak and dejected.

That evening, Gerald again begged her to stay on, appealing to her loyalty, telling her that they'd never get anyone to replace her, especially at this point in the season.

'Maybe I'll be able to find someone for you,' she offered. 'I'll write to the college where I trained, they might know of someone who's looking for a job.'

'A student's no good to me,' Gerald exclaimed. 'I've got to have someone who's experienced.'

'I didn't mean a student. The college often acts as a sort of employment agency for old pupils.'

'Promise me that you won't leave us in the lurch,' he entreated her. 'At least promise me that.'

'All right,' she agreed with a sigh. 'But you've got to promise to look out for someone as well.'

So they agreed to compromise, and that evening Romily wrote off to her old college giving details of the job, making it sound as attractive as possible, although she didn't think there was much chance of finding anyone who would be willing to work in such a remote place.

She didn't see James or try to phone him for the next two days, but she knew that she would have to make her mind up about him soon; he wasn't the kind of man who would let the situation go on indefinitely. He would want her again soon and then he would come looking for her. The following morning she was standing in the kitchen, gazing into nothingness, wondering whether or not to call James and what she would say to him if she did, when Carol came into the room.

'My dear Romily, how pensive you look!' she

observed with her artificial laugh. 'What's the matter, is James getting tired of your rather obvious charms? You really shouldn't be so eager, dear, it always puts a man off.'

Romily turned to face her, suddenly filled with hate. 'Well, you should know,' she pointed out acidly.

Carol's eyes narrowed in open dislike. 'You've refused to believe me all along, haven't you? But I assure you that James only used you so that he could come here and see me again. Oh, he knows I won't leave Gerald now, but he had to come and ask me one last time.'

'Really? When?'

'When we were alone together for those few minutes during the party,' Carol replied smoothly. 'Don't you remember? I sent you into the kitchen to go and start serving the food?'

'My God, Carol, you're a liar! James wouldn't touch you with a bargepole, and you know it!'

Her sister-in-law bristled angrily. 'You think so? Well, what if I proved to you otherwise? What if I rang him up and told him to meet me?'

'He wouldn't come,' Romily scoffed. 'He wouldn't even speak to you.'

'No? Well, let's find out, shall we?' And Carol strode over to the phone on the wall. 'You see,' she said as she dialled, 'I don't even have to look up the number, I know it off by heart.' After a moment someone answered the phone and she said, 'I'd like to speak to Mr Gordon, please. It's Mrs Bennion. No, *Mrs Carol* Bennion.'

Romily gazed at her, waiting for James to refuse to speak to her, but after only a short time Carol gave one of her cat-with-the-cream smiles and said, 'Hello, James.' Again Romily expected her to be cut off, but she went on, 'Darling, I've changed my mind. I've decided I will do what you want, after all. When? Now, if you like. Why, at our old meeting place, of course, over at the island. No, darling, it's there or nowhere. See you shortly then, darling.'

Putting down the phone, she laughed at Romily's appalled face. 'I did warn you, didn't I? As you saw, I only had to lift a finger.'

'I don't believe you,' Romily burst out. 'It wasn't James you were talking to. He wasn't on the other end of the line.'

Carol laughed delightedly. 'Oh, ye of little faith—or too much faith, in James's case. Come and see for yourself. You do know what his boat looks like, presumably?'

For a moment Romily was too stunned to move, but then she ran after Carol as she went down the garden and stopped in the screening shadow of a huge rhododendron bush just coming into flower, its buds full to bursting with mauve petals. There Carol waited, watching the island. Romily stood beside her, still not really believing, until a few minutes later they saw James's boat coming fast across the lake and steering towards the island.

'You see,' Carol laughed. She turned a triumphant face towards the younger girl. 'James could make do with you when he knew that I wasn't available, but now he'll drop you for the little tart you are!' Laughing again, she turned and ran down to the jetty, jumped into the boat and sped across to the island where James had tied up his boat and was waiting.

As Romily watched in sickened horror, James helped Carol out of the boat and the next second she was in his arms, clinging to him for a long moment before they both turned and went into the house.

Romily's legs gave way under her and she slumped down at the foot of the bush, the feeling of betrayal again flooding her, only twice as painfully this time. She tried to tell herself that it was a trick, but she had heard every word that Carol had said to him, had seen them embrace with her own eyes. Maybe it was true, maybe James had been using her to make Carol jealous, to drive her back to him. She longed to get as far away from them as possible, but some forlorn hope held her where she was, staring at the house on the island as her tortured mind pictured all that might be happening there. Were they making love. Were they discovering the delight in each other's bodies that they had known before?

It was almost an hour before they came out, Carol walking jauntily ahead of James. They got into their boats and left separately as they had come.

Romily ran back to the house and up to her bedroom, snatched up her car keys and ran down again, taking two or three stairs at a time. Gravel went flying up from her tyres as she accelerated the car up the driveway, and the postman's van coming down the other way had to swerve to avoid her. She drove so fast that she reached the boathouse at the same time as James did and jumped out of the car to run on to his jetty. 'You louse!' she yelled at him as he jumped on to the jetty with the mooring line in his hand. 'You rotten god-damned liar! I hope she makes your life hell!'

She began to run back towards her car as James shouted, 'Wait!' and hastily wrapped the mooring rope round a bollard. 'Romily, wait!'

But she had got back into her car and he had to leap out of the way as she shot forward, turning to go back towards the road.

'Romily!' He started to run after her, but she put her foot hard down and tore up to the road, turning into it on screeching tyres without even bothering to look to see if the way was clear. Her anger carried her on down past the turning to Abbot's Craig and for a couple of miles further along the narrow road before the tears started to come. Her foot eased off the accelerator and she realised where she was. She had no idea where she was going but she kept on driving anyway. What the hell else was there?

It was a few minutes later that she noticed the car coming fast down the road after her, and recognised it as James's. Immediately the fury returned a hundredfold and she pressed her foot into the floor, sending her little car bucketing down the steep hillside, taking the bends on the wrong side, her hands shaking with rage as she held the wheel, her eyes still full of tears. She didn't turn into the next bend until it was too late and hit the roadside with a sickening thud. She screeched to a halt and ended up with the front of the car half buried in the hedge. Romily scrambled out, her heartbeat suspended with fear, vaguely aware that James, too, had screeched to a halt and was getting out of his car.

A few seconds later he was beside her. 'Get in the car, Romily.'

'Go to hell!' she shouted furiously.

'All right but you're coming with me.' She started

to run, but he easily caught her and swung her over
his shoulder.

'You swine—put me down!'

She beat at his back as hard as she could, but he
merely dumped her into the car and held her there
while he got in himself, then drove quickly back
towards the castle.

'Let me out of here!' Romily yelled at him, and
tried to bite his hand. 'Why don't you go back to
your beloved Carol?'

James cursed and drew up in the castle courtyard
with a jerk. 'I don't want Carol. *You're* what I want,
God help me!' And lifting her out of the car he
carried her kicking and shouting across the drawbridge, through the main hall and up the stairs to
the bedroom with the huge four-poster bed. He set
her down on her feet, but she immediately began to
kick and hit out at him, using her nails to try and
scratch his face, shouting abuse at him through
tears of rage.

'For God's sake, you little vixen! Will you be still
and listen to me?'

'No! No, I hate you. You worm—you rotten liar!'

'All right, don't then,' James yelled back, his
patience suddenly snapping. 'But maybe this will
get to you!' And he began to tear at her dress.

'Oh!' Romily gave a gasp of stunned surprise and
began to fight him in earnest, but she was no match
for his strength, especially now that he was angry,
and he soon picked her up and dropped her on to the
bed, pinning her arms above her head, his weight
on top of her. 'Now will you listen to me?'

'Why the hell should I?' she shouted. Then, on an
angry despairing note, 'How could you just go to her

when she ordered you to like that? How *could* you?'

James's blue eyes grew harsh. 'Just what do you think we were doing out there?'

'Making love, of course. What else would Carol want you for?' Romily retorted furiously, trying to hurt.

'Why, you little . . .' He glared at her menacingly, his jaw thrust forward. Disgustedly, he said, 'I don't think you're ever going to learn to really trust me.' At that she turned her head to look at him and he said bitterly, 'I went there to meet Carol because on the night of the party I'd asked her to sell Abbot's Craig to me. Today, after a lot of haggling, she agreed.'

Romily's mouth fell open as she stared at him 'You're— you're going to buy her out?'

'Yes. With the proviso that she doesn't live within a hundred miles of here.'

'But—but what about Gerald? Will he agree?'

'He doesn't have much choice; Abbot's Craig was left to Carol by her father. She can do what she likes with it. Personally all I care about is the two of them getting as far away from us as possible.'

Romily gazed up at him, her eyes searching his face. Slowly she said, 'I was watching when you met Carol at the island. I saw you take—take her in your arms.'

'No,' James corrected shortly. 'You saw her grab me. All I did was try and push her away. At the time I thought she'd just done it to annoy me; I didn't realise it was for your benefit.' He looked down at her, his eyes not so angry now. 'What did she say to you?'

'That you'd asked her to go back to you. That

she'd refused but she was going to phone you and tell you that she'd changed her mind. I heard her when she called you; it sounded exactly as she'd said. And then—and then I saw you holding her. . .'

'It wasn't true. It wasn't like that,' he said urgently. His eyes darkened, grew intent. 'This is what is true.' And lowering his head, he took her mouth in a kiss of hungry passion.

It was several wonderful minutes before he let her go and Romily opened her eyes to look dreamily into his. What she read there made her aware that her dress was torn from their fight earlier and revealing bits of her in the most tempting places. James had noticed it too and his hands began to take full advantage of the fact.

'James,' she said rather breathlessly, 'do—do you remember that you said you only used this bed on special occasions?' He murmured acknowledgement, his mind elsewhere and she gave a gasp as he found her nipple, but went on, 'Have you had many women in it?'

He lifted his head, his blue eyes dancing with laughter. 'Do I denote a touch of jealousy?'

Romily hit him on the shoulder. 'Yes, you beast! I'm jealous as hell. Well, have you?'

As he looked down at her the laughter died and his face grew serious. 'No, I've never had a woman in this bed. Including Carol, before you ask. The special occasions were my birthdays—and they were damned lonely times.' He paused, then said deliberately, 'The only woman I'll ever sleep with in this bed will be the girl I love, the girl I intend to marry. If she'll have me.' His blue eyes gazed lovingly into hers. 'Will you have me, Romily, my love? Will you share my bed, and my life, and my future?'

'Oh!' She said the word on a long sigh of wonder and happiness as she put up her hand to gently touch his face. 'Do you really love me?'

'With all my heart and soul. Now and always.'

Misty tears filled her eyes, but she blinked them away and said practically, 'How about your body?'

James grinned delightedly. 'Definitely that, too.'

And as he began to show her just how much, the old four-poster bed became the witness to the first of many, many special occasions.

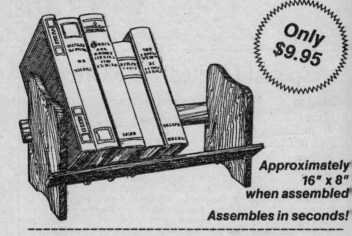

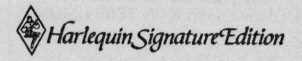

Harlequin Signature Edition

Carole Mortimer

Merlyn's Magic

She came to him from out of the storm and was drawn into his yearning arms—the tempestuous night held a magic all its own.

You've enjoyed Carole Mortimer's Harlequin Presents stories, and her previous bestseller, *Gypsy*.

Now, don't miss her latest, most exciting bestseller, *Merlyn's Magic!*

IN JULY

MERMG

All men wanted her,
but only one man would have her.

Her cruel father had intended
Angie to marry a sinister cattle baron twice her age.
No one expected that she would fall in love with his
handsome, pleasure-loving cowboy son.

Theirs was a love no desert storm would quench.

**In August
Harlequin celebrates**

The **1000**th

Presents

Passionate Relationship

by
Penny Jordan

**Harlequin Presents,
still and always the No. 1 romance
series in the world!**

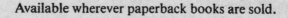